ÀDARA

5.9/5.0

ADARA

Beatrice Gormley

EERDMANS BOOKS FOR YOUNG READERS
GRAND RAPIDS, MICHIGAN / CAMBRIDGE, U.K.

© 2002 Beatrice Gormley

Published 2002 by Eerdmans Books for Young Readers
an imprint of Wm. B. Eerdmans Publishing Co.
255 Jefferson Ave. S.E. Grand Rapids, Michigan 49503
P.O. Box 163, Cambridge CB3 9PU U.K.

Printed in the United States of America

02 03 04 05 06 07 7 6 5 4 3 2 1

Library of Congress Cataloging-in-Publication Data

Gormley, Beatrice.
Adara / written by Beatrice Gormley.
p. cm.
Summary: A slave girl convinces her master, the mighty Syrian general,
Naaman, to seek a cure from his leprosy from the prophet Elisha in this
novelization of the Old Testament story.
ISBN 0-8028-5216-5 (alk. paper)
[1. Slaves—Fiction. 2. Naaman, the Syrian—Fiction. 3. Elisha (Biblical
prophet)—Fiction. 4. Bible—History of Biblical events—Fiction. 5. Syria—
History—To 333B.C.—Fiction.] I. Title

PZ7.G6696 Ad 2002   [Fic]—dc21   2002021609

Cover illustration by Tim Ladwig
Cover design by Matthew Van Zomeren

*In memory of Lew Mills,
who brought Bible stories to life for me*

The Setting for Adara's Story

It is the middle of the ninth century B.C.E. in ancient Israel. King Ahab of the Omrid Dynasty rules from his capital city of Samaria. Through his queen, Jezebel, he is allied to the Kingdom of Sidon, northwest of Israel on the Mediterranean seacoast. Religion in Israel is confused. With King Ahab's approval, there are many shrines to the Sidonian god and goddess Baal and Asherah, as well as to Yahweh (Jehovah). Many Israelites think of "Baal" and "Yahweh" as different names for the same god.

Off and on Ahab wages war with King Ben-Hadad of Aram, to the northeast. A bone of contention between Israel and Aram is the town of Ramoth-Gilead, where Adara and her family live. Ramoth-Gilead, an important stop on the trade route between Egypt and Mesopotamia, is under Aramean control for the moment.

Now King Ahab is leading his army across the Jordan River to take back Ramoth-Gilead for Israel. The armies of Damascus, commanded by General Naaman, are marching south to oppose him.

The Old Testament account of Naaman and Elisha is found in Kings II, Chapter 5.

Chapter 1

A Blast of Trumpets

I woke at dawn to a blast of trumpets. This would be my last day of freedom, but I had no idea of that. I was only sorry we were all crammed together on the rooftop of our house in town, instead of sleeping in the sweet-smelling vineyards. Our family included my father, Calev; my stepmother, Galya, and her two little children; my grown half brother, Dov; Dov's wife, Hannah; and our housekeeper, B'rinna (not actually a relation, but still part of our family). Then there were all the hired workers and their families.

Again, trumpets. I sat up on my sleeping mat. That was not the trumpet they blew from the town gates at sundown and sunrise. It was a whole chorus of trumpets outside the walls of Ramoth-Gilead.

"The battle!" exclaimed Dov, scrambling to his feet.

"Father, it is starting."

Within a few moments everyone else on the rooftop was up. Shading my eyes like the others, I stared at the eastern hills. The early light showed tents dotting the terraces where we had picked grapes yesterday afternoon. Something like a herd of thousands of cattle was moving over the slopes.

"The Aramean army is attacking," said Dov.

"Lord God Yahweh, save us," prayed B'rinna. "Holy Elisha, save us."

"We will be safe enough," said Father. "The Arameans are attacking the Israelites, not us. King Ahab must have brought the Israelite army into our wheat fields, although we cannot see them from here." Turning to Galya, he patted her shoulder. "Dov and I will go to watch from the town wall. We will return for the evening meal."

Galya's lip trembled, but she held up their baby, Guri. "Kiss your *Abba* good-bye, Guri." To Father she said, "The battle will be over by sundown, will it not?"

Father shrugged. "Who knows? The grain harvest is in, we can be thankful for that. We will have plenty to eat, even if the battle drags on for a week. And if the cisterns run dry, there's the underground well."

I pricked up my ears. The underground well. I knew of it, but I had never been allowed to go down there.

"I hope it does not come to that," said Galya. "What if we went down there for water and met soldiers?"

Hannah gasped at the thought. "They might find

4

the passageway that leads under our walls and follow it."

Father made a brushing motion, as if sweeping aside foolish fears.

"This is not a siege," Dov explained to the women. "The armies are fighting over Ramoth-Gilead, not against us. They know that after the battle, the town will open its gates to the victor. Is that not so, Father?"

Father nodded. "If you want to tremble," he told Galya and Hannah, "tremble for our vineyard. The heavy-footed Aramean army is camped right in the middle of it. Well, *shalom*, peace, then." He raised his hand at the family in farewell.

"*Shalom*," I chorused with the others. Weeks later, I would go over and over this scene in my mind, examining it as if it were a wall painting. I would think, there goes my father down the steps from the rooftop. There goes Dov, the good-natured half brother who taught me my letters. All I have of them now are memories.

Dov embraced Hannah and hurried after Father. He chanted a battle song as he disappeared down the steps:

> *When you marched out, Ba'al,*
> *The earth trembled, yea the heavens shook.*
> *The clouds shook water, the mountains quaked.*

For weeks there had been rumors of war between King Ben-hadad of Aram and King Ahab of Israel. A few

5

days ago a Phoenician merchant from Damascus, the capital city of Aram, had halted his caravan in our vineyards to dine with Father. I had listened to the men talk as I served them. Or rather, I had listened to the merchant Huram talk. Father sat without saying much, as usual.

Huram's thin, mobile features and dramatic gestures had told as much as the words he spoke. "Pick your grapes quickly, my friend." The merchant held up a warning finger. "General Naaman and the Aramean army are only a day or so behind me. And King Ahab is certainly on the march from Samaria, to seize Ramoth-Gilead for Israel." He sighed heavily. "We men who make an honest living are always at the mercy of the mighty, is that not the truth? If Israel or Aram are not making trouble in the land, it is Assyria, or even Egypt."

Now I sighed, too. Girls and women were even more at the mercy of the mighty, I thought. The men among the hired workers were following my father and Dov to the town walls. Meanwhile, we women and children had to wait at the house, crammed together like goats in a pen.

"Battle or no battle," said Galya, "there is water to be drawn and grain to be ground." She looked around the rooftop as she spoke, but especially at me.

I knew quite well, without Galya reminding me, what my first chore of the morning was. I climbed down the steps to the courtyard and drew water from the cistern. Stale water, stored there since the winter's rains. Ugh. I set the water jug down at the open edge of the kitchen, where strings of garlic hung from the lintel post. Nearby the wife of one of the workers had begun to grind flour for new bread.

Galya seemed to have forgotten about giving orders, for the moment. She sat at the bottom of the steps, sobbing to B'rinna and Hannah. "What if he is killed?" (She must mean Father.) "What if the town is sacked, and my little Guri" — she clutched the baby to her chest — "sold into slavery?" Galya's three-year-old daughter, Lila, clinging to a fold of her mother's tunic, whimpered.

I tapped a string of garlic to make it swing back and forth. "Slave traders would not buy babies."

B'rinna, sitting beside Galya and stroking her hair, looked at me with a warning finger against her lips. I bit my tongue. Not because I was wrong — obviously slave traders would want someone young enough to have a lot of work left in them, but not so young that they needed much care. But that would not be a comforting thought for Galya. Enemy soldiers would not therefore spare the babies. They would slaughter them.

"Now, now," B'rinna soothed Galya. "Remember what the master was just saying? Ramoth-Gilead is not fighting with either side. We need only keep safe until the fighting is over. If the Aramean army wins, we will open the gates. If the Israelite army wins, Governor Saadiah will have to flee to Damascus, but we will still

7

open the gates."

As Galya's sobs quieted, B'rinna went on, "Of course you are nervous, Mistress Galya. That is natural, since you gave birth so recently. Mothers always worry about their children. Did I ever tell you about the time the holy man Elisha saved my sons from slavery?"

Chapter 2

To the Tunnel

I had heard that story of B'rinna's many times. "Come, Lila." Picking up a basket of grapes, I led my little half sister back up to the rooftop. "We will make raisins." This should cheer up Lila, who loved sweet things.

One section of the flat roof was taken up with the loom and the bundles of fleece waiting to be combed and spun and woven. The rest of the space had been covered with sleeping bodies last night, but now the pallets were rolled aside. I showed Lila how to spread bunches of grapes out to dry.

Standing up to move the basket, I looked out toward the hills again. Both the armies were out of sight now, although dust kicked up by their feet and hooves was rising from the valley. The view in my favorite direction, north, was mostly blocked by the governor's mansion. But I could see a bit of the main north-south road, the King's Way, rippling over the hills.

Northward from Ramoth-Gilead stretched the best grasslands. Father's second son, one of my half brothers, was out there somewhere, working with the cattle herders. The Yarmuk River, the border between Gilead and Bashan, ran through these pastures, although it was hidden by the folds in the land.

If a traveler started out from Ramoth-Gilead and followed the King's Way north, he (or she! I thought) would cross the Yarmuk River and the high pastures of Bashan. He would travel on past Mount Hermon, topped with snow even at this hottest, driest time of year, and enter Aram. On the fourth day perhaps, the traveler on the King's Way would reach Damascus, where King Ben-hadad ruled. These days Father (and all the landowners of Gilead) paid taxes to Damascus, although we usually spoke Hebrew like the Israelites.

Of course King Ahab and Queen Jezebel of Israel wanted Gilead to pay taxes to Samaria instead. They needed more ivory beds for their palace, B'rinna said bitterly, and more costly purple robes. I did not say so to B'rinna, but I longed to see such a fabulous palace.

Damascus . . . Samaria! Sometimes I repeated the names of distant cities under my breath, just to put myself into a feverish state. If I were Queen Jezebel, I thought daringly, and could do whatever I liked, I would order a great caravan for myself. I would set out on the King's Road, and I would follow it north even beyond Damascus, across the Eastern Desert to Babylon.

I let Lila set out the last bunch of grapes. "You can chase the birds away from our grapes," I told my half sister.

"Go 'way, bird!" shouted Lila into the sky.

I smiled, and then I saw the bird — not a grape-stealing sparrow or blackbird. That bird up there, floating over the town on outstretched dark wings, was a vulture. It was watching the battle. Although I shivered, I wished that I too could watch the battle. But no one could see the battle from the town, unless they were standing on the walls like the men.

B'rinna called us to breakfast, and I took Lila back down the steps to the courtyard. Galya would send the workers' sons to take turns on the roof, scaring the birds away with their slings.

The morning dragged on. Over the noise in the courtyard, I listened to the faraway rumbling and thudding, the shouts, the clash of metal on metal. If King Ahab and General Naaman were not making war outside our walls, I thought, we could be out in the vineyards. We would be piling the two-handled baskets with bunches of grapes and carrying them to the stone vat. As the laborers trampled grapes, their legs purple to the thighs, we would all sing the merry wine-pressing songs.

I used to think of the year as a wheel that turned in

11

place, bringing the wine festival around every summer. Each month was like a spoke in a wheel of a cart. I had begged Dov to show me how to write the names of the months. He had drawn a circle in the dirt and scratched letters for each month, reciting their names.

Adar, the month of my birth, also came around each year, and so did the lambing season and Passover. So each year was the same — and yet each year was also different, I had begun to see. The wheel of the year did not spin in one place; it rolled forward.

Last harvest time Galya had not even been pregnant. This year she had watched the grape harvest from under a canopy with her new baby boy, Guri. For as many summers as I could remember, we had celebrated the wine festival in peace. This year we had fled the vineyards with the harvest only half-picked and hurried into the walled town with a few jars of grape juice and a few baskets of grapes.

Slowly the shadows in the courtyard grew shorter. Just before midday, one of Father's workers returned to let the women know about the progress of the battle. I listened as he told B'rinna, Galya, and Hannah. "The fight is fairly even so far. At first the Aramean archers had the advantage. But then the battle moved toward the town — "

" — and then it was the Israelite archers who were shooting from above," I finished, pleased that I understood. Galya frowned at me. I supposed she thought I should be more modest, especially in speaking about men's affairs. But if I worried every time Galya frowned at me . . . !

When the midday meal was ready, I ate my share of barley stew from the common bowl. Then I grabbed another round of bread and went off to the edge of the courtyard. A boy named Yanir, who had just come down from chasing birds on the roof, joined me in the thin strip of shade cast by the wall. I tore a piece from my bread and offered it to him.

Tucking his sling into his belt, he took the bread. "Listen to the battle now! It must be right outside the town."

I nodded, propping one elbow on a lamp-niche in the wall. I could hear the low blast of a ram's horn and the brighter note of a trumpet. "If only I were a man, I could watch from the walls."

"If I were a vulture," said Yanir with his mouth full, "I could watch from the sky." He laughed so hard at his own wit that bread crumbs fell out of his mouth.

Scowling, I chewed in silence for a moment. Then an idea struck me like a gust of wind. "The passage-way! We could take the passageway to the underground well and out to the spring to watch the battle from there."

"Ah, no — not me," Yanir drew back. "The master would beat me raw for that."

He was right, of course, but a demon of mischief had gotten into me. "Well, of course, if you are afraid . . . "

His face reddened. "I might be afraid of the master,

13

but you are afraid to go through the passageway by yourself."

"I am not at all afraid of the passageway." In fact, I felt almost pulled toward the cool, dark tunnel.

Chapter 3

Underground and Free

Yanir looked shocked at my boldness. "You would not dare." He laughed nervously.

"Watch and see," I said with a smile. I was afraid of Father too, but who would tell him? Yanir would not tell. Galya, Hannah, and B'rinna would soon be taking their midday nap with the rest of the household. Already some of the women were putting up a canopy in the courtyard and unrolling mats.

No midday nap for me! I would be off on my adventure. All I needed was a light for the tunnel — and there was an oil lamp, in the niche by my elbow.

I swallowed the last of my bread, trying to look unconcerned, as if my skin were not tingling all over. Like Yanir, I was shocked at my boldness. But now that I had said it out loud, I was determined to go into the tunnel. First, I had to get a live coal from the hearth.

B'rinna, strands of springy gray hair waving around her face, was baking a few last rounds of bread. I found a chipped clay dish, knelt beside her, and poked a red coal onto the dish. "Someone outside the gate needs fire," I explained.

B'rinna smiled at me as she pushed a strand of hair back under her headscarf. "You are a good, kind girl." That too was a sight I would remember later — B'rinna's face creased with wrinkles, but with something young and innocent about her eyes. "Do they look hungry?" she went on. "Offer them some bread, too. Your father wouldn't mind."

Forcing an answering smile, I tucked a round of bread into my sash. I was not a good girl, but I did not want B'rinna to worry about me. And she would not worry, I told myself, if she did not know where I was going. With a little luck I would not be missed at all.

Back at the courtyard wall I picked up the lamp. "*Shalom*, Yanir." I enjoyed the look on his face — fear mixed with admiration. In an unhurried way, I lifted the bar and slipped through the gate.

Out in the narrow lane it was hot and crowded and noisy enough to make our house seem cool and peaceful. Farm workers in loincloths and herders in goatskins were camped under makeshift awnings, along with their bundles, their cook-fires, and their families. Even if Galya had been up on the rooftop — which of course she was not, in the heat of the day —

16

she might not notice me in this crowd.

Threading my way through the crooked streets, I was soon out of the part of the town I knew best. I hoped I would recognize the tunnel entrance when I came to it. I knew it was in the side of a steep slope with vines growing over it.

In truth, I did not know much of the town, since girls were not supposed to go out by themselves. More and more often these days my stepmother reminded me of that, as well as of other things that well-brought-up girls did not do. But sometimes, when Galya was busy, B'rinna would send me to a neighbor's to borrow a measure of grain or a pinch of salt. Then I would steal the chance to look around a bit.

I had seen the governor's mansion, built of stone on the highest point in the town. Although I had never been inside the governor's house, Dov had, with Father. He said the mansion had more than eight rooms, not counting storerooms and stables. The reception hall was grand, with cedarwood pillars from Lebanon and enough chairs for several guests.

The town was as hot as a bake-oven this afternoon, and it seemed to grow hotter as I made my way down a steep, winding lane. There were fewer trees here, and the houses were small and mean, without courtyards. Refugees from the countryside crowded these alleys, too. The smell was bad, and I noticed heaps of garbage that no one had bothered to throw over the city walls.

Was this the place? I stopped in front of a rocky bank

at the back of a row of houses. Withered creeper vines hung over the rocks. Behind the vines, I could make out a darkness — yes, an opening in the bank.

With the brittle vines crackling, I ducked through the opening. I breathed in a cool earth smell. At the thought of being so well hidden from watchful eyes, I giggled. Even if Father walked down the street right now, he would never guess I was so close by.

Stooping in the low-roofed tunnel entrance, I tipped the dish with the coal to touch the wick of the lamp. The oily wick caught, and a dim glow lit the rocks on either side. Now! Lifting the lamp, I started carefully forward.

The lamp cast its light only one step's distance in front of me. As I went along, the roof of the passageway grew higher, and I straightened my back. The passageway was so narrow that I could have stretched out my right hand with the lamp and my left hand with the dish and touched both walls. The tunnel led downward, slanting this way and that.

After a little while, my mind seemed to grow cool and quiet like the passageway. Thoughts began to come out, like underground stars. When the battle was over, I mused, ordinary life would go on, but it would not be the same life for me.

If I were a boy, I would take up a man's work. Father would send me off to spend a year or so with the cattle herd, or maybe to join a merchant's caravan and travel to Damascus and back, learning about trade. I had

18

heard the Phoenician merchant Huram suggest that to Father for Yosef, his second son. Or I might join General Naaman's army.

But I, Adara, daughter of landowner Caleb ben Oved, was not a boy. Father would look around for a suitable husband for me. I was not old enough to marry, but I was almost old enough to become betrothed. Maybe to one of the governor's sons, as my stepmother had hinted.

Galya seemed to relish the thought of my marriage. Sometimes she sang the wedding song that had been composed for the wedding of King Ahab and Queen Jezebel many years ago:

Hear, O daughter, consider, and incline your ear;
forget your people and your father's house;
and the king will desire your beauty.
Since he is your Lord, bow to him . . .

B'rinna did not like this song any more than I did, although for a different reason. "That was an evil day, when King Ahab took Jezebel of Sidon to be his wife," she muttered.

I knew that Jezebel had done many evil things, but she gave me hope that maybe my own life would not be quite as dull as Galya's or Hannah's. Maybe I could find my own ways to have adventures. This afternoon's adventure seemed like a good start.

I paused. Was there something different about the

sound of my footsteps? I raised the lamp. Gasping, I let go of the dish with the coal. I was at the very edge of a steep drop.

The passageway had widened into a cave, almost filled with a pit as big as our courtyard. A spiral of steps led down the pit's limestone walls, and the shards of my dish scattered over the steps. Below, black water reflected the lamplight. "The hidden well," I breathed. Thank Yahweh that I had dropped the dish, not the lamp — and that I had stopped short of the pit.

Edging my way around the well, I found a shallow trough sloping down toward the cave wall. I lowered the lamp and saw where the trough disappeared into a tunnel. That must be where water ran out of the well when it was full.

I got down on my hands and knees and peered in. With the lamp in one hand, I would have to crawl three-legged. How much farther was the spring outside the walls? It was hard to judge time underground, but I was afraid the women might be waking from their naps. Still, I had come this far, and I would not stop now.

Cramped as I was in the tunnel, it seemed free and open compared with the future that waited for me. I felt like a quail being driven into a net. Maybe I could avoid marrying the governor's son, but I did not see how I could avoid marrying. If I flung myself before my father and let my tears drip onto his feet, he would probably allow me to choose not to marry a person I detested. He might even agree to try to arrange a marriage with a person I liked, if there were any such man.

But what if I tried to explain, "I do not know what I want, but I am afraid marriage would be the end of it. I have . . . longings. I want to learn to read — not just spelling out one word at a time as Dov does, but reading like a scribe, as fast as if I had already memorized the writing. And I want to travel, to see the snow on Mount Hermon in the summer and King Ahab's ivory palace in Samaria and the endless stretches of water on the Great Sea."

I could imagine my father staring at me, puffing out his breath in disgust. "Scribe! Ivory palace!" Then he would betroth me to the first man the matchmaker brought him, for sure.

Inching along, I rounded a bend in the tunnel, then another. My knees and my left hand were getting sore from crawling on the stone. The air down here seemed stale. I began to wonder if I would have to go back, after all — to crawl uphill and backwards to the well.

The lamp flared, then dimmed dangerously. How much oil was left? I had not thought to check it before I left the house.

A sudden gust up the passageway, like a warm breath, blew out the light. I stopped crawling and crouched there, trying not to scream.

Then I noticed a faint grayness in the dark around me. Over my hard breathing came the noises of thudding feet, rumbling wheels, clashing metal. I must be near the battle.

I crawled forward again quickly, and the darkness faded until it was only shade. One more turn in the passage, and the tunnel widened and ended in a pile of rocks. Beyond the rocks, clouds of dust blurred the sunlight. Soldiers surged around the huts outside the town.

Cautious as a jackal cub venturing out of its den, I set down the lamp and crept up to the pile of rocks at the entrance. Just as I peered over the barrier, a shower of stones hit the ground in front of the cave. Grit sprayed in my face. I flattened myself.

As soon as I got up my courage to look again, I realized that the stone-slingers had been aiming for a line of archers between the huts and me. At the blast of a horn the archers released their bowstrings, and arrows flew down over the fields in a cloud. An answering flock of arrows sped uphill at them. A few of the men staggered and fell, and one arrow clattered on the stones near the tunnel.

I flinched and shrank down behind the rocks again. Why had I come?

Chapter 4

Thunderbolt of Hadad

General Naaman rode easily as his golden chariot jounced over the stubbled wheat fields of Ramoth-Gilead. He was a strong man in himself, as mighty a warrior as any between Babylon and Egypt. Today he felt as strong as the warhorses that pulled his chariot. No, he was far stronger than that! He was as strong as the entire army of Aram, for it obeyed his every command.

The Israelite army had the advantage right now, slinging stones and shooting arrows downhill from the high ground outside the walled town. But the advantage would shift as the Arameans pretended to pull back, luring the Israelites down to the plain. Then Naaman would call his men to attack full force. The archers would rain down arrows until the Israelites broke ranks. After that, the Aramean swordsmen and horsemen would rush in and finish the Israelites off. Naaman, acting through his army, would strike like a thunderbolt from the hand of Hadad the Mighty.

The only drawback to this plan was King Ahab, who commanded the Israelites. He was a tough, wily old soldier, and he might see what the Arameans were up to. But where was Ahab?

Now and then, through the dust, Naaman spotted the Israelite standard, the bronze snake on its pole. But he could not see the splash of purple that would be Ahab's kingly robe. Naaman had spoken to the archers personally last night, urging them to aim for King Ahab. "If Ahab is slain, the Israelite army will be like a bronze snake without a head."

The standard of Aram, the pole topped by a golden calf, was fixed to Naaman's chariot. At any time during the battle, the Aramean soldiers could look for the standard and know that their general was with them in the thick of the fight. Arrows hummed past Naaman like deadly hornets, but he did not flinch. His men fought fearlessly because they saw him without fear. They could see that the god of battle loved their commander.

Naaman squinted across the battlefield, a lake of dust. Spear tips flashed, as many as reeds in a lake. At the back of the Israelite army a pair of horses reared up, pawing the dust — horses pulling a chariot. Perhaps that chariot carried Ahab in his purple robe and his helmet with iron horns, but Naaman could not see him. The Israelite king always wore iron horns in battle. They were said to bring him victory. A slight smile curled Naaman's lips. "Today victory is mine, Ahab."

"My Lord Commander?" asked the chariot driver. He thought the general was talking to him.

"To the left flank," Naaman told the driver. The driver touched the horses with the reins, and they wheeled to the left, the chariot plunging after them. Naaman's blood seemed to hum in his veins.

Chapter 5

Captured

I picked up the lamp and looked into it. It was still half full of oil. If only I had not dropped the dish with the live coal into the well!

I peered above the pile of rocks again. I knew this cave was not far from the town gates. If only the fighting would move downhill, I might be able to run behind the huts and around to the gates unnoticed.

Of course, the gates were shut and barred for the battle. I remembered the sound of the huge brassbound oak gates closing yesterday evening with a deep thud and clang. Would the gates open for me? Father was up on the wall, and he would see me. He would order the gatekeepers to open.

Or perhaps he could not. And even if the gatekeepers were willing to open for me, it took a long time to unbar the gates and push them out. I had watched the gatekeepers open the town one morning this spring, as our family was waiting to go out to the wheat fields.

Maybe they could lower a basket from the wall for me. I had heard stories of this being done, but I did not like the idea. I imagined crouching inside a hamper, waiting to be hauled up the town wall — shrinking from the whir and crackle of arrows piercing the wicker.

I looked down at the lamp again. There was a long, blind journey between me and safety. But if I kept one hand on the wall of the passage, surely I could find my way?

Find my way into the well, more likely! Remembering the black water glinting far down in the pit, I shivered.

Carefully raising my head above the rocks, I thought I might be able to run to the gates. As soon as the battle moved downhill, I would make a dash for it. The soldiers probably would not notice me even if I went now. It was just that I might get hit by stray stones and arrows.

No, in the din of thudding feet and hooves and clashing spears and shouts and screams and groans, the soldiers would not be likely to hear a girl calling to the watchers on the walls. The armies were so busy fighting, they might not even notice when the gate opened and closed. And for now, it seemed that I would be safe here in the shadow of the cave.

So I settled down to wait. Outside, the afternoon sun beat down on the dust-blurred battlefield. Waves of leather-helmeted foot soldiers rushed at each other, brandishing spears and roaring curses. The chariots charged after them, horses neighing, wheels clattering. From the rear, slingers kept on hurling a hailstorm of stones. Little by little, the Israelites seemed to be pushing the Arameans downhill and away from the town. I decided I would try for the gates as soon as both armies were below the ramp that led up from the valley.

Meanwhile, I shifted my position on the stony ground and wished Dov were there to explain the battle to me. Maybe he could point out the famous General Naaman. The merchant Huram had told my father that Naaman was such a hero as had not been seen for many years, a mighty warrior and beloved of all.

It was hard to guess the time of day, with the dust changing the light and the familiar valley of Ramoth-Gilead turned into a battlefield. Was B'rinna preparing the evening meal by now, and looking for me to chop onions or mind little Lila? Maybe Father would be coming home to eat. How foolish I had been, to think I could sneak out and return before anyone noticed!

Calev ben Oved, my father, did not shout and rage at his children when they disobeyed, the way some men did. But he always punished them, and today's disobedience would earn me a serious punishment. I might be forbidden to go out of the house again until my betrothal.

Looking at the slope to the right of the cave entrance, I noticed a shadow that had not been there before. I recognized the notched edge — it was the shadow of the tower at the town gates. It was getting late. The fighting was not moving any farther away.

If anything, the battle had drifted back closer to me. A band of Israelite archers was retreating up the slope, through the peasants' empty huts. One man was so close that I could almost count the arrows in his quiver. He shot arrow after arrow, as steadily as if he were at target practice.

Then, out of nowhere it seemed, an enemy arrow stabbed under the bronze scales of his armor. His bow slid from his hand as he fell into the dust, clutching the feathered shaft in his belly. I gulped and pressed my hands to my own stomach.

Looking away, my eyes locked on a chariot dashing out of the cloud of dust. Beside the driver a spearman watched his chance to stab, and a shield bearer thrust his shield out to protect him from arrows. I made a choked noise, pointing — did they not see the foot soldier lunging with his sword at their horses' hind legs?

With a scream the near horse fell, thrashing. He pulled down the second horse, the chariot toppled, and all three men sprawled in the dust. In an eyeblink the foot soldier was on top of the charioteer and cutting his throat, as neatly as a priest sacrificing a dove.

I felt sick. I felt guilty, as if I had watched something

forbidden. I closed my eyes for a moment.

Everywhere now Israelite soldiers were falling like stalks of wheat in the harvest. Another chariot rattled past the huts, the driver shouting something over and over in Hebrew. His passenger was slumped against one side, bouncing with the jolting chariot.

Then I understood the charioteer's words. "The king is dead! Retreat!" Others took up the cry. "Retreat!"

The Arameans chased the Israelites among the huts, hacking with swords. I forced my gaze down to the pebbles in the dry stream.

When I looked again, a soldier was running through the huts, waving a torch. Flames leaped up from the roofs. Through the shouting and crashing, someone began to roar out a song in Aramean. The words I caught were "Victory!" and "Loot!"

Should I make a run for it now? No. The town would never open the gates, with soldiers looting outside.

I felt queasy, and my forehead was cold with sweat. I could not stand to think of spending the night here — of spending one more moment here. Peering out of the cave, I noticed a hut nearby, falling apart as it burned. A pole toppled from a lean-to, breaking into pieces and scattering sparks. There was a light for my lamp.

I wanted so much to move, to do something. A flood of energy ran through my arms and legs, and I scrambled over the rocks and dashed out of the cave.

Moving at last! I felt better at once. I fastened all my attention on the short distance downhill to the broken pole. Stooping, I seized a stick by its unburned end. How easy! I almost laughed.

"Ho!" exclaimed a deep voice behind me.

I whirled. The laugh died, and my heart seemed to beat in my throat. A soldier as large as the giant Goliath blocked my way. Beyond his leather helmet loomed the town gates, with a red sun hanging over the towers. The cave entrance — suddenly far away — showed between the soldier's boot-clad legs.

My knees wobbled. "Let me by," I squeaked in Hebrew. Even as the words were coming out of my mouth, I realized how foolish they were.

The soldier seized my left wrist. "Ho, Niv! A good catch," he called in Aramean, to someone farther down the slope. "An Israelite maid." With a deft twist he bent my left arm behind my back and struck the firebrand from my right hand. Too late, the idea of thrusting the burning stick in his face flashed through my mind.

The soldier heaved me over his shoulder as if I were a spring lamb. "I am not Israelite!" I screamed, this time in Aramean. I beat his back, hurting my hands on metal-scaled leather. "Let me go! I am Gileadean! My father is Calev ben Oved! Help! Help! Help!"

Chapter 6

Naaman's Victory

The battle was over. At a word from Commanding General Naaman, his chariot driver reined the horses to a standstill. The day was over, too, with the blood-colored disk of the sun sinking into the haze above the town gates.

Naaman had known some time ago that the battle was as good as won. He had known it the moment he heard the swordsman's news. This man, fighting hand to hand with an Israelite, had gotten drawn into the enemy army without realizing it. Killing his foe after a fierce struggle, he had glanced around to get his bearings. Nearby stood a chariot, and there was something odd — the driver held the reins tight, although the horses shook their heads and pawed.

A man leaned against the inside of the chariot. He

stood upright, but only because he was tied to the rail. Blood seeped onto his kilt from a wound just beneath his breastplate. Under his helmet with iron horns, his face was as pale as death.

The Aramean swordsman realized at once that this must be Ahab, king of Israel. Hacking his way back to the Aramean lines, he found General Naaman. "No purple robe, but I swear I saw the iron horns, sir! It is King Ahab, badly wounded."

Naaman nodded. "He propped himself up in the chariot so his men would not lose heart." Naaman would have done the same thing, if he had been wounded.

The news about King Ahab spread through the Aramean army, and the troops surged forward. The Israelite troops also heard that their king was dying, and they began to fall back. Finally they fled from the gates of Ramoth-Gilead and scattered for the western hills.

Letting his officers direct the care of the wounded and the counting of the dead, Naaman paused for one of his rare quiet moments. After the frenzy of battle, he felt solemn. It was a serious thing, to act as the wrath of Hadad the Mighty. King Ahab must have feared that wrath, for he had not worn his kingly purple robe into battle. He had tried to hide from the Storm-god, but Hadad's arrow had found him just the same.

Now Ahab was dead, after ruling Israel for more than twenty years. King Ben-Hadad of Aram would be well pleased with Commanding General Naaman, for Israel would not be so quick to pick a fight with Aram again. King Ahab had two sons, but neither of them had the strength of Ahab. Queen Jezebel did, of course, but she would have to share power with her son, the new King.

Naaman beckoned to his aide in a nearby chariot. "Let the waiting messenger be sent to Damascus." There was no need for the general's scribe to write a letter for the messenger to take to King Ben-hadad, because the message was only one word: "Victory."

"And let every soldier be given extra wine tonight," Naaman told the aide. The army deserved to celebrate. They had fought well and bravely for the glory of Aram. There would not be much loot for them, since Aram was defending Ramoth-Gilead, not attacking it.

. . .

The next morning, while the Aramean army prepared to return to Damascus, Naaman and his officers rode their chariots into Ramoth-Gilead. The townspeople cheered from the walls as Naaman entered the gates. Beyond the gates, though, the procession was disappointing. The lanes of Ramoth-Gilead were too narrow for two horses to walk abreast. Naaman had to step down from his golden war chariot and walk the rest of the way to the governor's mansion.

Naaman was not much impressed with the Governor and his so-called mansion, or with the chair that the governor offered him. But he knew that the ceremonies after a victory are important. First the governor and his councilors had to greet and thank General Naaman with elaborate courtesy.

Then each landowner had to step forward and announce what he would send to Damascus, in gratitude that the town had been saved from the Israelite army. The governor spoke first, promising some fine pieces of brass from his personal stores. Most of the tribute was wool and wine, although some landowners also gave sheep, goats, or oxen.

The listing of the tribute went on and on. Each landowner went into detail about exactly what he was giving: not simply "six sheep," but "three ewes, a yearling ram, and two lambs." Not only "fifteen jugs of wine," but "six jugs of the wine of two years ago, together with one hundred bunches of raisins." And the landowners had to speak slowly, and sometimes repeat themselves, so that the Aramean scribe could write down each item. Naaman yawned.

One of the last landowners to speak listed his tribute, finishing with ". . . and 500 measures of barley, together with 267 measures of threshed wheat." Then he bowed again to Naaman. "Lord General, please accept the apologies of my neighbor, Calev ben Oved. He greatly desired to greet you today and thank you for saving his fields and vineyards from the evil Israelites (may Hadad curse their land and their generations to come). It is Calev's pleasure to send to Damascus ten great jugs of the best wine of his vineyards and forty fleeces of his finest white wool. But he could not be here, for a sorrow has fallen upon his family. A child, a daughter, died yesterday."

"My condolences to Calev ben Oved and his family," said Naaman. "But how could it happen that the child of a landowner was killed in the battle?"

"Her death had nothing to do with the battle, my Lord General," said the governor. "It was an accident in the town." He added, "Yes, her death is a sorrow for Calev ben Oved. But at least it was not a son that he lost."

The men in the hall, both townspeople and Arameans, murmured agreement. Naaman himself had two sons, and he knew it would be an unbearable grief to lose either one of them.

Chapter 7

A Lamb Among Wolves

My captor loped down the ramp, veering this way and that to avoid fallen bodies. I tried to scream, but my breath was jounced out of me with every step. Behind the walls and rooftops of Ramoth-Gilead, the setting sun disappeared in the smoke. If there were watchers on the gate towers, I could not make them out.

"Niv, you old vulture, there you are." The soldier carrying me paused to call to another soldier, pulling earrings and bracelets from one of the dead.

The man called Niv glanced up, and his mouth dropped open. He tucked the jewelry of the dead Israelite into his belt and straightened. "You lucky son of a jackal. I am wasting my time on copper trinkets, but you — what have you got?"

The soldier who looked like Goliath lowered me to my feet, keeping a tight hold on both my arms. "What do you think of this?" he asked. "Will the traders in Damascus not pay a good price for her?"

"My father is Calev ben Oved!" I gasped, getting my breath back. "He is on the council of Ramoth-Gilead. He knows the governor!"

"Shut your mouth, you," said "Goliath," giving me a shake. "I am going back to camp," he told his friend. "I have my booty." He swung me over his shoulder again and trotted on across the littered battlefield.

"No! No! No!" I screamed. I could not believe this was happening to me, Adara. If I denied it with all the force of my will, I could turn back the wheel of time. I had not dashed out of the cave. Or, I had prudently watched and waited until it was safe to dash out of the cave. Maybe I had retched my stomach empty, staying in the cave — so be it. Now I was willing to be sick, if only I could turn time backward.

But time kept rolling forward. My captor carried me across the fields and up into the hills. It was almost dark by the time we reached the Aramean camp, but I recognized the stubby outline of my father's watchtower. I was back in the very vineyard that I had been so sorry to leave yesterday afternoon. There was a musky scent of trampled grapes, along with the reek of sweaty men and camels. The campfire where "Goliath" stopped was a blazing pile of grapevines.

For just an instant, a wave of fury blotted out my

fear for myself. The army had ruined our vineyards. There would be no wine festival at Ramoth-Gilead next year.

Then "Goliath" set me down, and his comrades gathered to look me over. I wanted to stop my legs from trembling, but I could not. I was a lamb among wolves.

The soldiers agreed that "Goliath" was a lucky son of a jackal. "I thought we would be allowed to sack the town," one man grumbled. "Then there would have been plenty of captives to go around."

It seemed that of all the people of Ramoth-Gilead, only I had been stupid enough to get caught outside the town. This thought was too much for me, and I burst out crying. I was in the power of these horrible men, and it was my own fault.

"Goliath" tied my hands with a thong and then ignored me, as if I were a bleating lamb. The soldiers bound up their wounds, cleaned their javelins, and ate supper. Then an enormous wine jug was delivered to the unit, and the men drank freely. They traded stories of exciting moments during the battle. "Goliath" roared out a few lines of the same song Dov had sung before the battle, only with the name of the god changed:

When you marched out, Hadad,
The earth trembled, yea, the heavens shook.

The other men picked up the song and tramped

around the campfire, bawling out,

The clouds shook water.
The mountains quaked.

I was the one trembling and quaking. Crouching at
the edge of the firelight, I tried to make myself too
small to notice. If one of these rough men took a
notion to pick me up by the ankles and dash my brains
out against a rock, it would be easy for him to do it. I
wished I had never listened to stories of what soldiers
did after a battle.

The soldiers made up new verses for the song,
telling what had happened in today's battle:

You guided the hand of the archer, Hadad.
The arrow struck Ahab of Israel.
The arrow pierced him under his breastplate.
Ahab's blood filled the bottom of his chariot.

Finally the wine seemed to make the soldiers tired,
and they began to wrap themselves in their cloaks for
sleep. "Goliath" fastened a leash from my ankle to his
belt and threw down a blanket for me to lie on.

The coarse weave against my face smelled strongly
of camel — it must have been used under one of the
animals' packs. I thought of the herb-scented pallets
that we slept on at home. But you are not at home, I
told myself. I tried to summon up the pride and will-

fulness of Queen Jezebel. You are here. What can you do about it?

I thought of the story of Jael, the brave woman of the old days who had driven a tent stake through an enemy general's head. I could not do that. But maybe I could untie my bonds and creep out of the camp.

My heart raced at the very thought of stealing through the camp, past the sentries. The full moon was so bright. But if I could only sneak out of the vine-yards and across the fields to the tunnel entrance, I would be safe.

Cramping my fingers to reach the leather knots on my wrists, I picked at them until my fingers were sore. It was no use. The knots remained as hard and tight as if they had grown together.

I would have to think of something else. In the morning, I told myself, I would call out to an officer and explain who I was. I would tell him that my father would pay ransom to get me back. I flushed in the dark, ashamed that I had brought this trouble on my family. How much would Father have to pay? Maybe as much as the bride price he would receive for me in a few years.

My father had tried to protect me. B'rinna had tried to teach me to obey. Even my annoying stepmother had given me good advice. But I had sneaked away from safety and done exactly what I wanted — like Queen Jezebel. If only I could undo my foolish act! Every mus-cle in my body tensed, as if by straining I could turn

41

back that uncaring wheel of time.

· · ·

I woke up to the usual pre-dawn sounds and smells — a donkey braying, smoke from a campfire, people's voices. From behind my closed eyelids I sensed the familiar lightening of the sky in my father's vineyard. I thought, for just an instant, that the last two days had been a nightmare.

Then a man close by yawned, with a noise like a bull bellowing, and my eyes flew open. My memories came back in a flood, like garbage washed down a lane by a winter storm. I truly was in the middle of the Aramean camp. A foot prodded my side. "Come on, come on," said "Goliath."

He untied my hands, but he kept the tether on my ankle. Stumbling sleepily, I let myself be led to the edge of the camp to relieve myself behind some bushes. I thought I would burn up with shame, but the soldier seemed to think no more of it than if I had been a goat.

Following "Goliath" back to his unit, I looked around for the fringed kilt and oil-combed beard of a nobleman. But all the men near by seemed to be common soldiers. I watched one of them giving water to the donkeys and camels. I was fiercely thirsty myself, my throat still raw from screaming last night. When "Goliath" motioned the man to set the bucket in front of me, I put my face down to it like an animal.

"Goliath" sat on the steps of our watchtower to eat

his morning bread. Since I was tethered to him, so did I. Only two days ago, I had run up these steps with a gourd of grape juice for the watchman. Then, the wheat fields in the valley had been blond stubble. Now, the armies had trampled our fields into dust.

On a rise in the middle of the valley perched my town, Ramoth-Gilead. From this distance the town looked something like a headdress, a rounded mound ringed by a wall with guard towers. The day before yesterday I had sulked at leaving the vineyards for the hot, smelly town. Today, if only I could! The town's refuse would smell like the Garden of Eden to me.

I noticed a line of chariots crossing the fields. The head of the line had reached the ramp to the town gates. My chest lifted with hope. Of course — now the town council would welcome General Naaman and honor him for saving Ramoth-Gilead from King Ahab, just as they would have honored King Ahab for saving them from General Naaman, if the Israelite army had won. Councilor Calev ben Oved would have a chance to ask about his daughter. By tonight, I would be back in my father's house — in terrible disgrace, of course, but safely home.

A thumping from a lower terrace drew my attention to a young soldier beating a hand drum. He was stopping at each group of soldiers with the same announcement. "Prepare to break camp. Prepare to march north."

The army was leaving now! I looked north, where

the King's Way appeared and disappeared in the folds of the hills, and my stomach flopped as if I had stepped off the top of the watchtower. The road to Damascus, so enticing to me yesterday, now seemed like a path to the underworld. "Sir," I said to my captor, plucking at the sleeve of his tunic, "you must not leave yet! Very soon my father will send out a ransom, much silver, as much as you — "

"Shut your mouth," said "Goliath," cuffing the side of my head. He went to pack his gear, dragging me along by the tether.

In a short time the Aramean army, except for General Naaman and his officers, was pouring steadily out of the vineyards and onto the King's Way. "Goliath" had me walk ahead of him, behind the unit's pack animals. I was not tethered now, but I was surrounded by soldiers, and there was no cover larger than a thistle bush on either side of the road.

At the crest of the first hill, I paused to glance back through the white dust raised by thousands of feet and hooves. I strained my eyes for a messenger from Ramoth-Gilead, running after the army with a bag of silver from Father to buy me back. Then another cuff on the head, harder than before, sent me stumbling.

"Keep moving, stupid wench," growled "Goliath."

His comrade, Niv, laughed. "She thinks you will not beat her, for fear of spoiling her pretty face for the slave trader."

Pulling me to him, "Goliath" pushed his hairy face

into mine. His breath reeked of stale wine. "Want to find out if I would beat you?"

"No, please," I whimpered. I had already seen that the road behind the army was empty.

As I trudged onward, the last familiar thing I noticed was our family tomb, set into the hillside near several other tombs. My mother's bones lay there. Ordinarily I did not think about her much, but now I wondered how she felt as she lay dying of childbed fever. Did she say to herself, "This cannot happen to me"?

Chapter 8

A Chance to Escape

The morning wore on, the sun beat down, and the dusty white road rippled ahead. For the first time, I wondered if Father had any idea what had happened to me. No one but Yanir, the boy with the sling, knew I had gone to the hidden well. And he might not tell, for fear of getting a beating.

At noon the troops rested under oak trees at the bottom of a gully. The creek was dry this time of year, but the soldiers had water skins. "Goliath" gave me water and a piece of bread.

While I chewed the bread, I thought that even if Yanir did not tell where I had gone, B'rinna knew I had taken a coal. And they would find the lamp missing from the niche in the wall. Galya, always quick to suspect some mischief from me, would guess before long where I had gone — where else in all Ramoth-Gilead would I need a lamp, in the blazing noonday sun? Soon, now, my father would catch up with the army, pay my ransom, and take me home. Even if he was too angry with me to come himself, he would send Dov with the ransom.

The afternoon seemed longer than the morning. Uphill and downhill went the King's Way, like the same stretch of road over and over. From time to time I was seized with panic, so that I had to bite my lips to keep from screaming. But most of the time, I felt numb, almost forgetting why I was walking this road.

In a dull-minded way, I began to look forward to the crest of each hill. As I trudged up the slope, I became hotter and hotter, and sweat rolled down my neck and under my tunic. At the top, there would be just a moment when I could stretch out my arms and let the breeze blow through my tunic. Then I would start downhill again, into the heat and dust. Once in a while I caught sight of a village or a flock of sheep on a hillside.

Late in the afternoon, a few soldiers left the line of march. They caught up with their unit again when the troops stopped to camp for the night. Two of the other soldiers carried a whole sheep on a pole between them. Niv shoved ahead of him a boy a year or so older than me. The boy wore a tunic of undyed wool and a sleeveless sheepskin jacket.

"Ho!" called Niv, grinning. "Here is my captive, and

here is our feast. Who is a lucky son of a jackal now?"

After tethering the boy to a tree, the men began to cut up the sheep. Niv handed me a water skin and motioned to the boy. He wanted me to wash his wounds.

I stared at the boy's battered face and arms. He must have put up a good fight. Moistening a corner of my sash, I stepped up to the tree.

"Who are you?" he asked as I dabbed a cut over his eye. He moved his bruised lips slowly.

I began, "I am Adara, daughter of Calev ben Oved of Ramoth-Gilead, and I — "

He interrupted me with a short laugh. "Are you really? Well, I am Ezra ben Nobody. And I'm going to be Ezra, son of trouble, when the master finds out I've lost a sheep."

I did not think much of his manners, but it raised my spirits that he could make a joke about being captured. "I thought you already were in trouble," I said.

As I sponged his scrapes clean, Ezra told me he was a shepherd from a village near Edrei. He jerked his head toward the northeast. This time of year, he had to take his sheep far up in the hills to find grazing. He had seen the Aramean army marching south a couple of days ago, and he had hoped they and the Israelites would all kill each other. But the soldiers had reappeared sooner than he expected. "If I had known, I would have driven the flock farther away from the road."

"That is just the way I was thinking last night," I said eagerly. "If I had known . . . " I told him how I had crept through the passage to the hidden well and watched the battle from the tunnel. Ezra listened without comment until I came to the part where I dashed out to seize the firebrand, as brave and proud as Queen Jezebel.

"Wait," he interrupted. "You were safely hidden in the tunnel, watching the battle. Then, for no reason at all, you ran out right in front of the soldiers?"

"Not for no reason — I ran out to get the fire for my lamp," I retorted. "I did not think there were any soldiers near the cave."

Ezra looked me up and down, then shook his head. "It is a good thing your *Abba* will ransom you. You would never escape on your own. As for me, I will be long gone tomorrow morning when they break camp."

His tone was insulting, but his talk of escape gave me hope. Was Ezra boasting to make himself feel better, or could he really escape? I leaned close to him, pretending to examine a bad scrape on his elbow. "Take me with you," I whispered. "My father will reward you."

The boy looked at me thoughtfully. "You remind me of my silliest young ewe, Hyssop. She has a habit of stumbling into a ravine and then expecting me to pull her out."

His words stung, but I supposed it was his right to scold me before he helped me. Our chance to talk was over, for "Goliath" ordered me to the campfire to turn the spit. The soldiers who had captured Ezra made him lie down, still tethered to the tree, and tied his hands and feet. I watched from a distance, wondering what he thought about escaping now, but his face was expressionless.

The soldiers slept heavily that night, full of mutton. I kept waking and then dozing off again, each time noticing the past-full moon farther toward the west. I did not want to be sluggish with sleep, or to awake with a cry, if Ezra tapped me on the shoulder.

The last time I woke, as the moon was low in the sky, I thought I heard a strange sound. It was only "Goliath" snoring — or was it? I thought I caught something else, a quiet sawing, under cover of the snores. I raised my head and twisted to look at Ezra's tree. He was still there, asleep as far as I could see.

But in the morning, Ezra was gone. Niv shouted and swore when he found the cut thongs on the ground under the captive's tree. "Demons take the sneaking jackal's whelp! Hadad curse him to the end of his days, may they be short and miserable!" Turning to the sentry, he roared, "What did you do, stuff yourself with meat and fall asleep on watch? We could have all had our throats cut."

The other soldiers laughed. "If your whole head was cut off, Niv, you would not miss it much," said "Goliath." "The boy must have had a knife. Did you not search him?"

I bit my lip to keep from crying. Ezra could have cut my bonds, too, but he had left me to the mercies of these soldiers. After I had begged him to take me! After I had let him compare me to a silly ewe! I almost wished I had told Niv that his captive planned to escape.

During the second day's journey, I saw a herd of cattle on a distant hill. Maybe that was Father's herd, and maybe Josef, my second half brother, was there. But he might as well have been in Samaria, for any good he could do me.

I had tried to tell Ezra I was Adara, daughter of landowner and councilor Calev ben Oved. But I was almost beginning to think that did not matter. The soldiers cared nothing about who my father was.

Ezra had not been impressed with my high status, either. Indeed, he seemed to think I was a weak, soft, foolish girl who did not deserve to be rescued. Or maybe he just thought I would put him in more danger, if he tried to take me along. Maybe he was right.

I saw now that Yanir, too, must have thought of me as a foolish girl who might put him in danger. Would he be tempted to escape punishment by pretending he knew nothing of what happened to me? After all, no one had heard us talk about the passageway to the hidden well.

The day of the battle had been a confusing time, with so many extra women and children in the house and Father and Dov away at the walls. If Yanir did not tell what he knew, if no one recognized the coal I had taken and the missing lamp as clues, Father and the others might not think of the passageway to the well. They might get the idea that I had gone off on my own and that something had happened to me in the town. They might search Ramoth-Gilead for a long time.

Galya says that demons whisper horrible thoughts to those who lie awake in the dark of the night. But my demons whispered to me in broad daylight, tormenting me mile after mile.

That afternoon, we crossed the Yarmuk River at a ford. The Yarmuk was the border between Gilead and Bashan. Now I was outside my homeland, two days' journey from my father's house.

Chapter 9

The Slave Market

Day after day I plodded along in a stupor. I was a girl without a family, without a home, without a town. I was nothing.

I could not believe that my life was turned upside down, and yet the sun kept rising and setting. The Aramean army crawled northward over the King's Road, and I was borne helplessly along in the middle of them. Wind sighed over the parched, tawny grass. We passed by two walled towns, not as large as Ramoth-Gilead.

Sometimes at a distance I caught sight of cattle in the shade of the oak trees that dotted the hills. But most living things, beasts and human, stayed well away from the army. Only vultures floated overhead, perhaps hoping for another battle. My thoughts narrowed down to the blisters on my feet and the passage of the sun overhead, marking the times to rest and eat.

On the third day the road began to climb upward. Rocks poked out of the dry slopes, and the oak trees gave way to scrubby pines. As I reached the top of one more hill, I heard "Goliath" remark to Niv, "Look, Mount Hermon. We have made good time."

To the west there was something different — a wall of blue mountains, topped with white. My heart thrilled, just for an instant. Surely that was the home of Ba'al the storm-god, or Hadad, as they called him in Aram.

"Glory be to Hadad!" "Goliath" and Niv raised their spears toward the mountain. "To the God of Thunderbolts belongs our victory." Behind them, other soldiers came into view of the mountain and shouted, "Glory be to Hadad!"

I had a thought that would have been comical, if it were not so painful. I was gazing upon Mount Hermon, as I had longed to do — but not because I was as rich and powerful as Queen Jezebel. I saw the mountain only because I was a captive, on my way to being sold as a slave. My plight reminded me of one of Galya's tales, about a foolish man whose wishes come true, but in horrible ways.

As we climbed higher into the foothills, the air was cooler. The sweet-smelling pine trees grew more thickly, casting some shade on the road. The next day the road turned east and followed a river downhill. The trees disappeared, except for oaks and sycamores along the river.

In spite of everything, I was eager to see Damascus. I expected it would be built on a hill, like Ramoth-Gilead, and like Samaria in B'rinna's descriptions. But when Damascus finally appeared, it was nestled at the bottom of the river valley. Past the city, the river disappeared into the ground, and the farmland stopped suddenly. Beyond that, desert stretched eastward as far as I could see.

Before we reached the outskirts of the city, "Goliath" stopped on the riverbank and had me wash my face and arms and pick the burrs out of my hair. Then he tied my hands in front of me. I wondered where he thought I would run, if I could get away from him.

Damascus was much larger than Ramoth-Gilead, but its walls were low, more like the courtyard walls at home than like the high walls of my town. We passed through the northern gate. Just inside, there was a market crowded with stalls and booths. I would have been curious to see the wares, if I had not been an item for sale myself.

We passed stalls with cages of fowl, then a section where sheep and goats were penned. Finally "Goliath" stopped at a pen of women and girls. The slave dealer, a heavy man with a sagging face, turned me around while "Goliath" talked me up. See how healthy I was! I spoke Aramean as well as Hebrew. I wove fine cloth . . .

That lie was almost amusing. Galya often nagged me about my unskilled weaving.

"She is from Ramoth-Gilead, eh, soldier?" asked the dealer as he squeezed my arm muscles. "You know the custom: the commander gets first pick of the captives from a battle."

"Goliath" looked alarmed, as if he had not thought of that. "No, not from Ramoth-Gilead at all. They did not let us sack the town. Some enemy soldiers were captured, but they were sold south right after the battle. This girl is from . . . Samaria."

"Hm." The dealer opened my mouth with his dirty fingers to look at my teeth. "Because if she was from Ramoth-Gilead, you really ought to show her to General Naaman. I do not want any trouble."

I hardly heard what they were saying, paralyzed as I was with shame. To be handled by a man, a strange man! (I had gotten somewhat used to "Goliath," and in any case he had hardly touched me, except to tie me up, since the first day's march.) Tears seeped out of my eyes as the two men haggled over my price. Finally the dealer took out his scales, weighed a small pile of silver pieces, and poured them into the soldier's hand.

As "Goliath" disappeared into the crowded market, the slave dealer began to order the girls and women to stand here or there. He placed me in a front corner.

"You probably think you are the best merchandise, you little vixen," muttered a woman behind me. She pinched my arm.

Just then there came a call from up the market street: "Make way for Lady Doronit, wife of General Naaman!"

There was a buzz among the slaves. A curtained litter appeared, led by a well-dressed man with an important air. He stepped up to the dealer. "I am Aharon, Lady Doronit's steward. She wishes to see the captives from General Naaman's great victory over the Israelites at Ramoth-Gilead and choose one slave, as is her right."

The slave dealer bowed low. "My lady brings great honor on my humble business. But has she not heard that the army returned with no captives from the battle of Ramoth-Gilead? The town was not sacked, and the captured enemy soldiers were sold south on the spot. Oh, would that I might offer to her ladyship the very flower of Gilead for her choosing! Yet I have a number of fine women and girls here, if she wishes to consider purchasing one. Did her ladyship have in mind a lady's maid, or a nursemaid, or . . . ?"

The other women and girls smoothed their tunics and pressed to the front of the pen. "Let me through!" whispered the woman behind me, pinching me harder. I squealed, but I stood my ground. If the others were so eager to be bought for General Naaman's household, I was not going to give up my chance.

The curtains of the litter opened, showing a woman with hair dressed in elaborate braids and ringlets. The gold beads on her forehead clinked as she leaned out.

"Aharon, I have no need of another slave, if I must pay for her."

At the sound of Lady Doronit's musical voice, my heart tripped hopefully. "Please, lady," I called in Hebrew, "I am a captive from the battle of Ramoth-Gilead."

The dealer sprang at me, cursing, and shoved me back so hard that I fell. The woman who had pinched me jumped to the front of the pen.

Chapter 10

Not a Slave

I sprawled on the ground among the other girls and women, scraping my elbow. Someone stepped on my hand, and I cried out. But I heard Lady Doronit ask her steward, "What did the girl say? Was she not speaking Hebrew, like an Israelite?"

As I struggled to get back in sight of the litter, I heard the dealer's oily voice go on and on. He tried to convince the steward that I was crazy, or a liar, or both. I was from Samaria, he claimed, and had nothing to do with the battle of Ramoth-Gilead. Furthermore, I was a sickly, unskilled wench who had given him no end of trouble.

"In that case," said the lady, forgetting to speak to the slave dealer through her steward, "you will be glad to have me take the girl off your hands."

"Let her step forward again," said the steward to the dealer. "Her ladyship's wish is as the wish of General Naaman, mighty commander of the King's army."

As the slaves moved aside to let me through, I saw the sour expression on the dealer's face. The lady, looking very pleased with herself, motioned me forward. "What is your name, little lamb?"

If anyone had called me "little lamb" last week, I would have found it hard to be polite. But this was the first kind word anyone had said to me since I left my father's house. I must please the lady, so that she would take me away with her.

"I am Adara, Lady." This time I spoke in Aramean. "Oh, please, please take me!" I leaned over the fence rail, trembling. If I had had a wooly lamb's tail, I would have wagged it.

The lady laughed. "What a sweet face! No doubt Raiza will scold me . . ."

Who was Raiza? I cast my eyes down, afraid to seem too bold. I waited.

"We will take the girl, as is General Naaman's right," said the steward's voice. I knew, though my gaze was still on the ground, that her ladyship had nodded.

With a light step I followed Aharon, the steward, away from the slave market. Once Lady Doronit knew who my father was and how I had come to be captured, a messenger could be sent to Ramoth-Gilead. Father would send my ransom, or perhaps bring it himself and take me home again.

After a long walk through the streets, we entered the outer courtyard of a villa grander than the governor's mansion in Ramoth-Gilead. I expected a chance to speak with the lady now and explain how I had been captured by mistake. But Aharon left me with the housekeeper. "Here, Raiza — a prize of the General's victory at Ramoth-Gilead," he explained, and he hurried after the lady's curtained litter. I was disappointed, but maybe Lady Doronit would send for me later.

Raiza was a woman of middle age, handsome except for the frown that creased her forehead. (I would learn that the frown was permanent, maybe because she was the one who had to keep the other slaves in line.) "What is your name?" asked the housekeeper as she untied my hands. She had brisk, raspy way of talking.

"I am Adara of Ramoth-Gilead, daughter of . . . ," I began.

"I know where you are from," the housekeeper's frown deepened as she cut me off. "I asked only what you are called. Sima," she beckoned to a girl crossing the courtyard, "take this new girl, Adara, with you on your rounds. She will watch and learn."

I opened my mouth to explain to the housekeeper who I really was, and that Lady Doronit would want me to be treated courteously. But then I shut my mouth. Maybe it was best to wait to straighten out the misunderstanding.

Sima, a girl with an angular face, gave me a sizing-up glance. I thought she was a little older than I was, but maybe it was only her knowing expression. Handing me the jar she was carrying, she beckoned me to follow. A passageway opencd on a second courtyard. This was not a service courtyard, but a garden of cool air and pink and white blossoms — oleander bushes. "Oh!" I exclaimed. A sparkling stream flowed right through the courtyard.

"Have you never seen running water?" Sima looked at me with amusement. "This stream flows through the kitchen courtyard, too."

The jar I was carrying contained oil, from which Sima filled the lamps in niches along the walls of the courtyard. She also dipped water from the stream and watered the shrubs and vines, talking as she worked. I let her go on, but I gazed around admiring the pictures on the tiled walls.

"Are you listening to me?" demanded Sima. "If Raiza happens to be watching you work in this courtyard and you do not bow to the household gods each time you pass the shrine, she will beat you. She is very pious. She is afraid of signs and portents, and she is always consulting the fortune-teller."

"I will not need to worry about Raiza," I said cheerfully. "I will not be here long. As soon as Lady Doronit knows who my father is, I will be going home. I am not a slave."

Straightening up with the dipper, Sima stared at me and gave a short laugh. "Oh, indeed! Did not her ladyship find you at the slave dealer's?"

"Yes, but — "

"Listen to me," Sima interrupted. "If you know what is good for you, you will not speak this way again, especially in Raiza's hearing. If she gets the idea that a girl is not of sound mind, she will advise Aharon to remove her from the household. You do not believe me? That is exactly what happened to poor Yoni, who walked in her sleep. Sold to a brothel."

A chill ran down my neck. I had felt almost safe in this household, as if the wife of the governor of Ramoth-Gilead had taken me in. But the fact was that until I could persuade Lady Doronit to send for my father, I was in the power of the housekeeper. And Raiza did not seem anything like our kindly B'rinna.

Finished with the courtyard, Sima took me back to the slave quarters and showed me the tiny room where she and three other girls slept. "Since you are the newest, you will sleep at the entrance, in case Raiza wants someone during the night. She suffers from rheumatism."

I hoped I would be able to speak to Lady Doronit before that, but I said nothing. It was almost evening now, and Sima led me to the kitchen courtyard, where the slaves ate. Just as Sima had said, a stream flowed along the edge of the courtyard. It filled a drinking basin, then a trough for horses and camels, then a pool for washing. So no one in this household had to drink stale water from a cistern or haul water from a well. When I drank, the water was cold and sweet.

After supper, Raiza beckoned to me, and I expected that now she would send me to Lady Doronit. Instead, she asked, "What can you do? Can you spin fine thread? Are you skilled at brewing herbal drinks? Tell me the truth, and I will not beat you for it."

"I can spin only coarse thread," I admitted. "And wait on guests at dinner. But — " In spite of Sima's warning, I burst out, "please let me speak to Lady Doronit! I must tell her who I am, and that my father will want to ransom me."

"Silence." The housekeeper slapped my mouth — not angrily, but just the way Father might slap a donkey on the muzzle, to remind it who was in charge. "You are not to annoy her ladyship with your silly stories. Get that through your head."

The other slaves were preparing to lie down for the night. I went to bed on the shabbiest pallet in the girls' sleeping chamber, my face stinging from the slap.

Chapter 11

The Procession

The next morning I was awakened by someone tripping over my pallet. "You need not lie right in the doorway, Adara," said a female voice.

My eyes not yet open, I struggled to make sense of this — the voice of someone who called me by name, someone who felt free to criticize me, yet it did not sound like Galya or Hannah.

"Hurry!" Now a woman's voice, a raspy one. All at once I knew that Raiza, the housekeeper, was outside the girls' chamber. I was in Damascus, and it was Sima who had tripped over me. "Her ladyship wants us in her courtyard," Raiza went on. "The general is in the hills above the city. He will enter the North Gate with a grand procession to the temple of Hadad."

I just had time to splash water on my face and stumble after the other slaves. Half asleep still, I thought with one part of my mind how unfair Sima was, first telling me to lie near the door and then complaining that I was there. With another part of my mind, I wondered what the procession had to do with the slaves.

In the garden courtyard the men and boy slaves were already assembled, blinking and yawning. Lady Doronit walked back and forth along the stream, almost skipping with excitement. Beneath the tasseled fringe of her skirt, her anklets chimed and her toe-rings gleamed. I could see that this was not the time for me to step forward and explain who I really was.

"Aharon," Lady Doronit told the steward, "hand out the timbrels to the women. Let them dance forward in a line — no, four abreast. Let them keep time with the timbrel as they shout, 'Hail, Naaman, the mighty leader of hosts!'"

After some fumbling and false starts, we managed to dance, beat our timbrels, and shout as Lady Doronit wished. Then she had the steward line the men up behind us, also four abreast. They were to answer us by shouting, "Hail, General Naaman, beloved of Hadad!"

Raiza looked worried at this, and I heard her say under her breath, "The god should not be tempted." But Lady Doronit did not notice. The men practiced their part, and then we all practiced together.

"Next after the men will come the soldiers," Lady Doronit went on. "They have already left for the hills. Then the officers, and the general in his chariot. And finally . . ." she paused, looking disappointed, "last should come the captives in chains. But it was not that kind of a battle, was it, Aharon?"

"No, my lady," said the steward. He waved a hand at me. "Only the one captive from Ramoth-Gilead."

Lady Doronit had to admit it would not be an impressive sight if only one girl in chains followed the conquering hero's chariot. So I would play the timbrel and dance and shout with the other slaves.

After more practice, Lady Doronit had Raiza pick oleander blossoms, which the women tucked into their hair. Then we returned to the kitchen courtyard for a quick breakfast. Lady Doronit appeared in her litter with two young boys, her sons. In the procession, they were to ride on the shoulders of two of the men. The younger boy, about five years old, kept shouting, "Hail, Father, beloved of Hadad!"

"Not yet, young master," Aharon told him.

We all followed her ladyship's litter through the streets. At the North Gate a crowd had gathered, and more people were pushing into it all the time. Aharon had to shout and shove with his staff to make way for the general's household.

Outside the city gate, we joined a throng of more women and girls, also decked with flowers and carrying timbrels. Aharon reminded General Naaman's slaves what they were supposed to do. "We dance up the road toward the army. When we meet them, we turn and process before them back into the city. Is that clear?"

I gazed at the hill above the city. The first ranks of spear throwers came into view, marching down the winding road. After them, rank upon rank of archers. And then —

"See, the general's golden chariot!" Sima pointed to the very top of the hill, where bright metal flashed in the morning sun.

Trumpets blared from the tower above the gates. A great shout, "Hail, Naaman!" went up all along the wall. I shouted with Sima and the women, "Hail, Naaman, mighty leader of hosts!" Behind us the men shouted back, "Hail, General Naaman, beloved of Hadad!"

We danced up the road, thumping our timbrels. Last year at the harvest festival I had danced and sung in the procession to the shrine in the western hills. But I had never been part of such a huge celebration as this one. Although I was there only because of a misunderstanding, I too was swept up in the festive mood.

When we met the army on the road, there was some confusion, because we had not practiced turning around. As we were milling about, with Aharon barking directions, Lady Doronit caught up with us. The litter curtains and canopy were pushed back, and she stood on the seat, holding onto the curtain frame. "I shall lead the procession into the city. Follow me!"

Her gauzy headscarf rippling in the wind, Lady Doronit chanted verses at the top of her lungs:

See his war horses prance,
fierce as the wind-steeds that pull
Hadad's cloud-chariot.
See, Naaman comes,
fierce as the Storm-god himself . . .

Raiza moaned as she made the sign to turn aside bad luck. "No offense meant to Lord Hadad the Storm-god," she muttered.

The rest of us chanted the chorus: "Hail, Naaman, mighty leader of hosts!"

The procession took half the morning to parade through the streets of Damascus. I was hoarse from shouting, and the palm of my hand was sore from beating the timbrel by the time we reached the temple of Hadad.

I had never seen a temple before, although I had heard of the temple King Solomon had built in Jerusalem. Broad stone steps led up to an open porch, where an old man in purple robes stood between two bronze pillars. I knew by his tall crown and his staff topped with the golden calf that he must be King Benhadad. Before we turned aside at the bottom of the steps, I caught a glimpse of carved gold-covered doors behind him. Those were the doors to the holy place.

I was curious to see the inside of the temple. Was it furnished with golden lamp stands and incense burners, like the temple of Solomon? But I knew that only priests and the most important worshipers were allowed in the sanctuary. Sacrifices were made out here, though, for we stopped near a great altar laid with firewood.

Like a forking stream of water, the procession parted to one side of the temple steps or the other. Last of all, General Naaman's golden chariot stopped before the temple. The general held up his arms to the cheering crowd, then climbed the steps and knelt before the king.

King Ben-hadad reached out his hand, raising the general to his feet, and embraced him. Then he beckoned for General Naaman to accompany him. At a stately pace they disappeared through the tall golden doors.

"His Majesty takes my husband into the inner temple, into the very presence of the god!" exclaimed Lady Doronit. Tears of joy ran down her face.

"Ah," murmured Aharon. "Surely the god loves our master." But Raiza put a hand over her eyes and shivered.

Then we returned to the general's villa, because the public part of the celebration was over. General Naaman would not come home until much later, I heard Lady Doronit tell the steward. The general would spend the afternoon and evening at the royal palace, at a banquet in honor of his great victory. "I am exhausted!" Lady Doronit went on. "How I have spent myself, rejoicing! I must rest. Raiza, have a light supper brought to my chamber."

Back at the general's house, we could hardly squeeze into the outer courtyard. It was filled with a train of pack animals.

"Tribute to General Naaman from the landowners of Ramoth-Gilead," the head camel driver explained to Aharon.

"Have a man take that camel — the King's portion — to the palace storehouses," said the steward. He motioned toward a camel laden with rolled fleeces and wine jars. "As for the rest, unpack the tribute and leave it in the courtyard. The general and my lady will inspect the goods in the morning."

I hardly heard Aharon's last words, because I was squinting at the landowner's marks on the bundles. As a driver grasped the camel's halter, I lunged at the leather strap around one of the fleeces. "The mark! It is Father's mark!" Burned into the leather was the letter *gamel* — for "Calev."

Sima grabbed my arm, trying to pull me back. "What has gotten into you, Adara?"

"My father's mark!" I shook her off. Pushing aside the fleece, I stood on tiptoe to peer at the top of a wine jar. The mark on the clay stopper — again, *gamel*. This was wine from grapes I had helped to pick. "My father has sent my ransom, in wool and wine! Sima, I am ransomed! Aharon — Sir — my father must have sent these goods."

The steward gave me a disgusted look, but he spoke to Sima. "Is she mad? Has she talked this way before?"

I turned to the head camel driver with clasped hands. "Did not Calev ben Oved give you this wool and wine to ransom his daughter, Adara?"

Sima clapped her hand over my mouth. "Be careful! I warned you . . ."

The camel driver squinted at me. "Ransom? No such thing. Councilor Calev sent the goods to the general as a gift, in gratitude that Ramoth-Gilead was saved from King Ahab, the Israelite." He added, "I heard that he did lose a daughter, now that you mention it, but not to the Arameans. She was a headstrong thing — she sneaked off to the hidden well under Ramoth-Gilead. Drowned down there."

"No! She did not! I did not!" I burst into tears.

Aharon shook me, and Sima brought a dipper of cold water to pour over my head. But it was some time before I could stop crying. It was as if my father stood here in the courtyard and yet did not see me. His wealth was here, but it had nothing to do with me. He thought I was dead.

Chapter 12

The Favorite of the Gods

"Lord General, another day has dawned in which it is my pleasure to serve you." Aharon, the steward, stepped into Naaman's bedchamber and bowed. "Will you come to the outer courtyard and inspect the gifts from the landowners of Ramoth-Gilead? The scribe has already gone over the goods with his list, and he says there are gifts over and above the tribute agreed upon."

Naaman did not nod, since his manservant was trimming his beard, but he lifted a hand. "Very good. I will come soon. Ask Lady Doronit to come view the tribute, too. She may do as she wishes with the gifts."

Although Naaman enjoyed the rough life of the campaign trail, he also enjoyed his comfortable home. It was good to be back with his wife and his two manly little sons. He had completed one more successful military campaign, the most successful one yet. He was beloved of everyone in Damascus, from the lowest beggar to King Ben-Hadad himself.

Now that Naaman had the tribute from Ramoth-Gilead, he did not care what was done with the goods. Above all, he wanted Doronit and everyone else to be as happy as he was.

The steward bowed again. "Lord General, I took the responsibility of sending a portion of the gifts to the warehouses of King Ben-hadad, may he live forever."

Naaman smiled at his steward. "Well done, Aharon."

After his hair and beard were combed with perfumed oil and the valet had pinned his mantle with a gold pin, Naaman went to the outer courtyard. Raiza was showing Doronit the tribute, but she paused to bow low to him. "Good morning, my Lord General, and welcome home."

Good old Raiza, always fussing around the household with that little frown on her face, as if she had the heavy responsibility of commanding the armies of Aram. Naaman chatted with her a bit, asking if her rheumatism was better and what she thought about the quality of the tribute wool. Meanwhile Doronit rushed from one bundle to another like a child surrounded by honey cakes.

"Oh, my Lord General!" His wife addressed him formally in front of the slaves, as was proper. "See, these ivory plaques from Sidon!" She held up one of a goddess gazing from a window, and one of the Tree of Life. "Shall we have a great bed made, like the one they say Queen Jezebel has in Samaria, its frame inlaid with ivory?"

"Just as you wish, my dear," he laughed. "We must do something with all these goods. They are cluttering up the courtyard."

Doronit stooped to inspect the objects the house-keeper was unwrapping. "And what are those bronzes, Raiza?"

"They seem to be lanterns — no, I believe they are braziers, my lady." Raiza rubbed one against her tunic to polish it and held it up to the sunlight. "Although I have never seen workmanship so fine." The metal filigree showed a hunter aiming his bow at a stag.

"And so many of them!" exclaimed Doronit. "Why, my Lord, we could warm our bedchambers, the nursery, and the dining hall. We could even place braziers around our garden in the cold season!"

"Whatever you like, my dear." Naaman beamed at his wife. It had been wonderful to see her at the city gate yesterday, wild with excitement at his triumph. Perhaps she had been a little indiscreet, jumping into the procession and singing a victory song to him. But he would not reprimand her and spoil her happiness.

"Oh, my lord," Doronit went on, "There is a new slave girl, a captive from Ramoth-Gilead. Would you like to see her?"

"A girl captive from Ramoth-Gilead?" Naaman was puzzled. "I did not expect any captives, since I was defending the town." Perhaps she had been attached to the defeated Israelite army.

Raiza went to fetch the new slave, and a moment later a girl of about eleven or twelve knelt before Naaman. She had a hesitant manner, almost stunned, but that was not unusual for one recently captured. He lifted the girl's chin with his hand. For a moment her eyes, large and wary like an antelope's, looked into his.

"Does she not have a sweet face?" Doronit asked Naaman. "True, we did not really need another slave girl, but I paid nothing for her. I think I will keep her to tell me stories as I spin.

"Oh, and my lord, what fine wool I will spin this winter!" Naaman's wife whirled toward still another bundle, a fleece, and pulled out a handful of the wool. "See how long and white it is! I will have a new shawl woven, white with a border of blue lilies." Turning again, she pointed to a wooden chest. "Only wait until you see the jewelry they sent. There is a pin, silver with lapis lazuli, that could fasten my new shawl."

Laughing, Naaman held up his hands. "Why not? All shall be as you have said." The girl did have a sweet face, he thought. She would soon settle into her new life, and it would be pleasant to have her around the house.

Chapter 13

Adara, the Slave

I am a slave. I am a slave. During the next few weeks, these words seemed to beat in my head all the time, as loud as the song of General Naaman's victory procession. I did not try to speak to Lady Doronit again, and she seemed to have forgotten about me. She was very busy these days, overseeing the arrangement of the braziers and other new furnishings and instructing the woodworkers who came to build the ivory-inlaid bed.

General Naaman's household did not need another slave girl, as her ladyship had said, but that did not mean I would not work. It meant that the other slaves gave me their dullest, most unpleasant chores. As I emptied slop jars into the gutter outside the gate or scrubbed Raiza's washing, I thought over what must have happened in the days after the battle. Yanir had told my family of my boast, and they had searched the hidden passageway to the well.

I imagined Dov lifting his torch above the steps leading down the side of the well. He would have found shards of the pottery dish, perhaps the dead coal. B'rinna would remember that it was the same dish I had taken. Father and the rest would think they knew what had happened to me — I had come upon the well suddenly and stumbled in. As indeed I almost had.

So I did not exist, in anyone's mind, except in Damascus — and here I was nothing but a slave. I must be very careful what I said and did. I must not displease Aharon or Raiza or even Sima, let alone Lady Doronit. As Sima had warned me, I could be sold into a far worse setting.

Still, I did not entirely give up hope. For now my family thought I was dead in Ramoth-Gilead instead of alive in Damascus, but that could change. Sooner or later, I told myself, the camel-driver who had brought my father's tribute would return to Ramoth-Gilead. Since everyone in the town gossiped about everything, especially anything remarkable that a stranger might say, my father would hear of the slave girl in Damascus who claimed to be the daughter of Calev ben Oved. Then he might guess what had actually become of me.

Washing dirty tunics in the courtyard stream, I imagined how it would be when Father appeared to ransom me. It could happen at any moment, even now while I was scrubbing someone's undergarment. My father would enter the courtyard and say, "Adara, my beloved daughter! They have made you do the laundry? Oh, my little dove!"

Tenderly Father would wrap me in a rich robe. He would fling a bag of silver at the steward as he led me off. And we would journey back down the King's Way, only this time I would ride on a donkey.

I told myself this story over and over. Each time, I had an instant of joy in which I was again Adara, daughter of landowner Calev ben Oved. But then the happy instant was gone. I was staring at the gray water of the laundry basin, my hands cold and sore. I was Adara, the slave.

Once when I was lost in my daydream, just at the moment I imagined Father appearing in the courtyard, I felt a tickling on the back of my neck. A bug — a spider? The tickling crept lower. I yipped and tried to slap my back.

Then I heard a giggle, and I turned to see the general's older son, Maimon, running back into the house. Maybe he feared I would slap him, but I would not dare. I was Adara, the slave.

Days went by, then weeks. I heard the steward mention to the housekeeper that caravans had left Damascus to cross the Eastern Desert. They would stop at the oasis of Tadmor on their way to Babylon. If the camel driver I had spoken to was in that caravan, he was traveling away from Ramoth-Gilead.

The harvest season passed, and the days grew cooler and shorter. Here on the edge of the desert, the wind had a sharper bite than in Ramoth-Gilead. The other slaves of the household put on their long-sleeved tunics, but I had only what I was wearing on the hot day I was captured.

Raiza gave Sima and me a new task: to keep the decorative bronze braziers burning in the rooms of the family's quarters. Soon the only time I was warm was the few moments that I carried a pan of live coals from the kitchen fire. I wrapped my headscarf close around me, but it was a thin summer scarf and not very large.

One day after the midday meal, Raiza told me that her ladyship wished me to come to her. "She is in the garden courtyard," she said. "Wait, comb your hair first."

I had no comb of my own, but I tidied my hair with another girl's broken-toothed comb and washed my face. Hurrying to the garden courtyard, I found Lady Doronit and her personal maids sitting on the benches, spinning. There was also a loom in one corner. The weaver's cloth, white with blue lilies in the border, looked almost finished.

The scene reminded me of the rainy season in Gilead, when the women at home spun the wool from that year's fleece. Except, of course, we could not sit in the garden because we had none; or even on the roof because the weather was wet. At this time last year, I had spent long, gray afternoons spinning with B'rinna,

Galya, and Hannah. Even my young stepsister, Lila, had her own grubby practice spindle.

I knelt before Lady Doronit (what a pleasant warmth came from the brazier next to her!) and bowed my head, "Here I am, my lady."

"Adara — you shall tell us a story of Israel," she said. "I am weary of the stories of Aram, I have heard them so many times."

I hesitated. I had certainly heard many tales from the women on those endless winter afternoons at home. But I was not sure those stories would entertain Lady Doronit — not all of them had entertained me very much. Galya told lesson-stories, like the one about the foolish man who wished for a mountain of silver. When his wish came true, he was crushed underneath the heavy precious metal.

Hannah liked to tell how she had come to be married to Dov. Just from catching sight of her at the well, Dov had gone mad with love for her. He had begged Father, with tears in his eyes, to hurry to Hannah's father with a bride price. I could not imagine Dov, stolid and practical like Father, getting so excited about anything. In any case, I did not think it was much of a story.

"Do the women in Ramoth-Gilead not pass the time with stories?" asked Lady Doronit, a sharp note in her voice.

"Yes, my lady."

I seemed to see B'rinna's kindly wrinkled face, her

81

eyes lighting up as she asked, "Did I ever tell you about the time the holy man Elisha saved my sons from slavery?"

I would tell that story.

Sitting back on my heels, I held up one hand, as storytellers did. "O gracious lady, hearken if you will to the story of B'rinna, woman of Samaria in Israel, and learn how her sons were saved from slavery."

Chapter 14

Saved from Slavery

Lady Doronit looked up from her spindle with interest. I remembered that she, like B'rinna, had two sons.

As I began the story, I seemed to hear B'rinna's warm voice in my ears, and the way she cleared her throat every so often. In my mind's eye I saw her shifting her legs, careful not to disturb Lila, who would often go to sleep against her. "This happened in the days when B'rinna's husband and Elisha were followers of Elijah, prophet of the Lord God Yahweh."

The woman at the loom spoke up. "A god named Yahweh? Are they heathens in Israel, then?"

"No, they worship Ba'al and Asherah," said Lady Doronit. "This must have been a cult. In any case, it is only a story. Continue," she told me.

"Elisha was the disciple closest to the prophet," I

went on, "and if any of the others wanted to ask Elijah for help, they would go to Elisha. In B'rinna's tale, it was about this time of year, and oil was high-priced in Samaria because the last olive harvest had been scant. Poor B'rinna could not afford to buy oil.

"That was a terrible, terrible year. B'rinna was a widow, for her husband had been beaten to death by Queen Jezebel's guards for preaching against her Baal-idols. When he died of his wounds, she screamed toward the sky, 'Lord God, why did you not protect your servant, my husband?'"

I, Adara, paused in my telling. Last year I had not thought much about Queen Jezebel's guards, but now I imagined them so clearly. They looked like "Goliath," the Aramean soldier who had captured me outside Ramoth-Gilead.

"So B'rinna was left with her two boys," I continued, "not much older than — " B'rinna used to say, "not much older than Adara," and she would reach over to pat my arm. In Damascus, there was no one to look fondly at me and pat my arm. I swallowed a lump in my throat. "Not much older than her ladyship's sons."

Lady Doronit nodded, pleased, and I went on with the story. B'rinna had to borrow money for food, but she could not pay it back. So the moneylender seized her land. Now he owned even her house. She borrowed again to pay rent on the house, and to buy a little jar of oil and a measure of barley meal.

"The moneylender, a cruel, hard man — " I now

imagined him as heavy, with pouchy eyes, like the slave dealer in Damascus " — came around. He told B'rinna if she did not pay all she owed, he would seize her sons for slaves. And he could do it, too, because King Ahab's judges said it was the law.

"B'rinna went to Elisha and begged for help. She hoped the prophet Elijah's band might have a little reserve of silver, enough to make a payment to the moneylender and put him off for the moment. But there was no money.

"'The prophet himself is fasting,' Elisha had told B'rinna. But he did not turn away from her. He stood in the doorway, looking at her with compassion."

When B'rinna came to this part of the story, her voice always grew hoarse, and now mine did, too. I described how Elisha had looked into her eyes, as if he cared about her troubles just as much as she did. That was worth all the gold in King Ahab's treasury, B'rinna always said.

"Then Elisha burst out, as if he was not even expecting to say it, 'Go borrow jars.'

"'Jars?' B'rinna thought she must have misunderstood him.

"'Yes, all the jars you can — every last jar in the neighborhood.' He shook his head, looking confused and excited. 'I cannot explain why. Just do it.'

"It made no sense to B'rinna, but she was frantic to do something so she obeyed him. What with the hard times, her neighbors had plenty of empty jars.

"After B'rinna had collected dozens of jars, Elisha told her to take her boys inside, shut the doors, and fill all the borrowed jars from her one small jar of oil."

"But that was impossible," interrupted the weaver. Lady Doronit frowned, and the woman said hastily, "Pardon, my lady. I spoke out of turn."

"Of course it was impossible!" I threw up my hands, just the way B'rinna always did. "Even so, if you had heard the tone of Elisha's voice, and seen his kind eyes . . . So, alone in her hut with her children, B'rinna poured oil into one of the empty jars. The strange thing was, her own jar remained heavy.

"B'rinna's heart beat faster. She motioned her older son to set aside the jar she had just filled and the younger boy to bring her another. Again oil flowed, and it filled the second jar. She continued to fill jars until every last jar brimmed and the fruity fragrance of olive oil hung in the room.

"Sobbing aloud with joy, B'rinna ran to tell Elisha what had happened. She saw tears come to his eyes. He danced right there in the street, with people staring and pointing at him. 'Great is the glory of the Lord!' he sang. 'Though the Lord be high, he cares for the lowly.' Then he calmed down and told her, 'Sell the oil, pay your debts, and live on the rest of the money.'"

My voice slowed, as B'rinna's voice always did to mark the end of the story, "And you can imagine that she did just that."

After I stopped speaking, the women worked in

silence for a moment. Putting my hands in my lap, I felt content for the first time in weeks. I was pleasantly warm, partly from the nearby brazier and partly because I had felt close to B'rinna while I told her story.

Lady Doronit chuckled. "A god who cares for the lowly!"

Her women joined in, "What an idea! How fanciful!"

"Well," said her ladyship, "I suppose there must be a god for everything."

Early the next morning, as Sima and I were filling pans with coals, Raiza came into the kitchen. "Girls, what do you think of my new shawl?" Beaming, she rubbed her cheek against the soft wool draped over her shoulders.

Sima's face lit up, too, and she burst out with compliments. It was a beautiful shawl — such fine workmanship — and how becoming to Madam Raiza! I saw that Sima had her eye not on the shawl Raiza was wearing, but the one she was carrying on her arm.

"Yes, her ladyship's new shawl was finished yesterday, and she graciously presented me with this one, hardly worn at all." Raiza smiled at Sima and held out the shawl on her arm. "And I give my second-best shawl to you."

Shrugging off her old shawl, Sima bowed and let out a stream of flattery on the housekeeper. Madam Raiza was as gracious as Lady Doronit! Surely the Great Mother Asherah would bless Madam for her generosity! Sima snuggled into Raiza's shawl and turned beaming to me, "There you are, Adara. A shawl for you, too!" She nodded at the cloth she had let drop to the kitchen floor.

My face burned as I picked up Sima's old shawl. I fingered the tattered fringe and looked at the stains. I had never worn anything so shabby, except when I did messy work like picking grapes.

Sima was looking at me, waiting. Before she could take offense, I forced out thanks. "You are gracious to me, Sima. I do not deserve such a gift." In order not to look her in the face, I pretended to admire the old piece of cloth. I murmured, "Your kindness has already warmed me, and the shawl will keep me warmer still."

Smiling, Sima adjusted the shawl around my shoulders. "If you fold it so," she said, "the largest oil stain hardly shows."

• • •

That night I dreamed that I was out in the desert by myself. I was barefoot and wearing only a thin tunic. I was frozen with fear. I was afraid to take a step in the dark — there might be scorpions, or I might stumble into a ravine. I heard a lion roar nearby.

I thought I was already as full of fear as I could be and still live. Then I heard footsteps coming toward me. I trembled. Surely it was someone who would do me more harm than scorpions or lions. I crouched down and made myself as small as possible, although there was no place to hide.

"*Shalom*, peace, Adara."

I looked up. Peace indeed flooded through me. The man before me was holy Elisha. I recognized him by his worn goatskin mantle and by his bushy eyebrows, but most of all by the deep kindness in his eyes. Light and warmth surrounded him, and now they were around me, too. There was nothing to be afraid of.

• • •

In the days following the dream of holy Elisha, I was surprised that the peace did not leave me. That dream was quite different from my daydream of being rescued by my father. The daydream was bright while I was caught up in it, but afterward my life as a slave seemed even drearier than before. But the peace of Elisha seemed to be with me even when I was not actually thinking about the dream.

I understood now why B'rinna had been willing to leave Samaria and come to live in Ramoth-Gilead. "Did you not want to stay near the holy man?" I had asked her once.

"Oh, yes, I would have liked that," she had answered, "but my road led to Ramoth-Gilead. Holy Elisha told me so." She had paused in her work, gazing to the west as if she could see Samaria beyond the hills. "Besides, his spirit is close to me even here."

Chapter 15:

Sima's Story

I gave up my daydream of being rescued by my father. My memory of him seemed as thin as smoke, and, anyway, my mind became busy with other things. I spent some time each day thinking about the story I would tell Lady Doronit, if she sent for me.

I thought B'rinna's stories were the best, and usually Lady Doronit seemed to agree. She liked the story of how the holy man Elijah had brought a child back to life by breathing into his mouth. She especially liked the story of Ruth, who had left her homeland because she loved her mother-in-law, Naomi, so much.

The story of Ruth reminded me of B'rinna herself, leaving her home in Samaria and traveling all the way to Ramoth-Gilead. According to Dov, she had simply appeared at our courtyard gate one day shortly after my mother had died. Holy Elisha had sent her to Calev ben Oved's house, she said. My father had tried to put her off, but he did need someone to care for the newborn baby (me) and run the household. Before anyone knew it, B'rinna had become part of our family.

Thinking of B'rinna, I was surprised when one of Lady Doronit's women said, "My lady is just like Naomi in that story. And we are just like Ruth — devoted to her ladyship until our dying day." I did not think Lady Doronit was anything like Naomi. But her ladyship was smiling in a pleased way, so I said nothing.

One day I told B'rinna's most exciting story, about how the shepherd lad David slew the mighty warrior Goliath. I thought anybody would enjoy the story of David and Goliath, but after I had finished telling it there was an uncomfortable silence in the courtyard. Then Lady Doronit laughed scornfully. "What a ridiculously far-fetched tale!"

The weaver was quick to join in, "Who wants to listen to stories that could never happen?" And Lady Doronit did not send for me again for several days.

When I told Sima how Lady Doronit seemed to dislike my story, Sima gave me a look. It was a look she often gave me, a look that said I was even stupider than she had thought. "Have you happened to notice, in the many months you have lived in this household, who Lady Doronit's husband is?"

"General Naaman, of course," I snapped. Then I

thought a moment. "Oh. General Naaman, a mighty warrior."

Sima rolled her eyes at my slow-wittedness. "Very good!" she said in mock admiration.

"But the giant Goliath was not really like the general," I protested. "Goliath was huge and boastful. He was not handsome or kind like General Naaman."

Before I finished speaking, Sima jangled the copper bangles on her wrist to show that my explanation was worth no more than such noise. "I would not put myself in a position where I had to explain those fine distinctions to the mistress."

I had to admit, I owed a great deal to Sima, even though she bossed me around and criticized me and made me do some of her work. Sima was a favorite of Raiza's, and sometimes Sima would share with me the little privileges she got from Raiza. For instance, Sima would take me with her on an errand in the city, such as fetching the fortune-teller for Raiza. Raiza was a great believer in this old woman who foretold the future, and she took her warnings seriously.

Lady Doronit sometimes consulted the fortune-teller too, but mainly for amusement. Her ladyship giggled as she asked questions such as, "What gifts will my Lord General bring me from his next expedition?" The fortune-teller gave fanciful answers that made Lady Doronit and her women laugh out loud.

Other times, Raiza might have Sima and me deliver a message from Lady Doronit to the wife of another general or go to one city gate or another to find out which caravans had arrived. On our errands Sima and I would always take a detour through the market. The first time we did this, I begged, "Let us not go by the slave pens, though."

Pausing in front of a leather-worker's stall, Sima stared at me. "Do you think I want to go by the slave pens? I would just as soon visit my mother, Asherah curse her."

I stared back. "Your mother is alive? In Damascus? Why do you not want to see her?"

Then, as Sima led me on through the twisted lanes to avoid the slave market, she told me her story. When she was six her father, who worked a small farm outside Damascus, had died in the pestilence. Her mother had married again, and soon Sima had two half sisters and a half brother. Her stepfather did not manage the farm well, and there was less to eat. One night Sima overheard her stepfather and her mother talking about how to make ends meet.

"She is growing like a weed and eating like an ox — only not hay," complained her stepfather. Sima guessed he was talking about her. Sure enough, Sima's mother replied with something about the bride price Sima would bring them, when she turned thirteen. "Hadad do so to me and more if I feed that snip three more years, waiting for the bride price," her stepfather growled. Her mother protested, but they talked on, and Sima did not hear what they decided.

A few days later, Sima's mother was especially affectionate with her. She washed Sima's hair in warm water perfumed with lavender. As they sat on the edge of the stone trough in the sunshine, with the mother combing Sima's hair and singing a little song, her stepfather appeared. Behind him rode a man on a donkey, a man with a face like a wineskin.

Sima had understood at once that the man was a slave dealer. She kicked and bit, but her mother held her by the hair while her stepfather helped the slave dealer tie her on his donkey. As the slave dealer took her away, Sima heard her mother sobbing, "There was nothing else I could do, Sima. When you are older, you will understand."

"I understand already, you false-tongued slut of a jackal's mother!" screamed Sima. The next day, she was a kitchen maid in General Naaman's household.

I was so shocked by Sima's story that I could hardly enjoy the market that first day. But as time went on, we came to the market again and again. Of course neither of us had any silver, but Sima sometimes sneaked a handful of spices or an extra lamp from the household to trade at the jewelry stalls.

I did not dare steal goods to trade, but what I liked best did not cost anything anyway. I would go to the scribes' corner of the market. Standing behind a scribe, I watched him write letters or contracts for his customers. I would try to guess, before the scribe wrote a word, how he would spell it out with his pen.

Those were free and easy times Sima and I had on our errands. At home in Ramoth-Gilead, I would have been in disgrace if I loitered in the market. As Galya used to tell me, no honorable man would want to marry a girl who made herself so public. Now Raiza might scold and slap Sima and me if she knew we were wasting time, but she cared not a fig who saw us in public.

· · ·

One morning Sima and I were grinding wheat in the courtyard. In time to the grinding, I sang a song B'rinna used to sing.

> *Yahweh is his name, rejoice before him!*
> *Father of orphans, defender of widows*
> *God in his holy habitation!*
> *God gives the solitary a home and*
> *brings forth prisoners into freedom,*
> *but —*

"Hold your tongue!" Sima was glaring at me. "It is bad enough to bend my back over a grindstone, without listening to your honeyed donkey-dung song."

If I had not heard how Sima's mother sang to her as the slave dealer approached, I would have been angry and hurt. But I only said quietly, "It is not donkey-dung. It is true."

Sima snorted, and we went on grinding. But later, as

we filled the lamps in the courtyard, she said suddenly, "Even if there is a god who cares for the helpless, he is an Israelite god. He is not in Damascus."

"Yes, he is," I said. "I know he is near."

"Hunh. Well, then — perhaps he cares for you, since you are an Israelite, more or less, and your foster mother is a friend of his prophet. But he would not care for a Damascan girl."

I felt worried, because I did not know how to answer. I was not a holy man. How could I, Adara, speak for the Lord God? But I could not stand to think that God would comfort me and not Sima. Finally I said, "I think he would."

Sima gave another snort and said no more about it. But that evening she came to me with a comb and sat down with her back to me. My heart beat faster as I gazed at the black hair rippling over Sima's shoulders. I began to comb, trying to be very gentle as I tugged the snarls out of Sima's curly locks.

After a moment Sima gave a long sigh and said, "Sing something."

I began a song about doves, but Sima interrupted me. "No, sing — sing, you know."

I could hardly believe what she wanted to hear, but I began timidly,

Father of orphans, defender of widows . . .

Sima sighed even deeper, and I thought I heard her

sniffle too. I sang B'rinna's song all the way through and over and over, until I had finished combing Sima's hair.

Chapter 16

An Ungrateful Daughter

The wheel of the year turned once more. My second winter in Damascus was more comfortable, because Raiza came up with a long-sleeved wool tunic for me to wear. Scanty rain sprinkled the brown hills above the city of Damascus, and the hills turned green. Then the rain stopped, and each day the sun shone hotter.

One afternoon, carrying a basket of flax to the garden courtyard, I halted my steps to listen. I heard men's voices at the other end of the corridor. "The Lord General will see you if you truly have words for his ears," Aharon was saying, "but I warn you that he has little patience. He leaves the household business to me and Lady Doronit."

"I did not come to the house of General Naaman to display wares," said the other man.

I gasped and turned to stare. It was not the words that shocked me. It was the man's voice, and the way he used his hands when he talked. I knew him! It was my father's friend, the Phoenician merchant Huram.

The two men disappeared into the reception hall, where the general saw visitors. I stood outside the courtyard, trembling. Was that really Huram, sent by my father, or was I deceiving myself again?

The steward left the hall and disappeared in the direction of the family quarters. Setting down the basket, I tiptoed to the door of the reception hall. Merchant Huram — yes, those were his thin, sharp features — waited on a bench.

I returned to the garden courtyard, shaking with excitement. I helped the weaver set up her loom, but I was clumsy today, and she scolded me. I paid no heed.

The merchant had come looking for me. I was sure of it. It was almost as if my old daydream was coming true. I would be rescued from slavery at last.

Lady Doronit appeared in the courtyard, and I sat down to spin with her and her women. After we had been at work for a short while, the steward appeared. I expected him to summon me, and I half-rose as he glanced in my direction. But he spoke to Lady Doronit. "My Lord General wishes my lady to attend him in the reception hall."

I waited for only a short time after that, I suppose, but my thoughts seemed to live through days and days. My mind raced to Ramoth-Gilead and back to

Damascus again. What if the general did not summon me, but only asked Lady Doronit if she were willing to let Huram ransom me? What if she objected? Huram was a well-to-do merchant, but he had no power to make the general release me.

At last Aharon stepped into the courtyard again and beckoned to me. He did not explain why I was wanted or speak as I followed him down the corridor. But he kept turning to glance at me, as if there was more to me than he had suspected.

In the hall Lady Doronit stood behind an openwork screen. From there she could speak to her husband in the presence of a stranger, but without being seen. I knelt beside her and waited to be told what to do.

The general sat on his carved chair, facing the merchant on his bench. "And the news from Samaria, my Lord General," Huram was saying. "After King Ahab's death at the battle of Ramoth-Gilead, his elder son, Ahaziah, ascended the throne of Israel. But not for long. Shortly before my last visit to the capital city, he fell to his death from a window."

"Yes, yes," said General Naaman. He rubbed one side of his jaw, and I wondered why his beard was uneven. "King Ben-Hadad (may he live forever) and his councilors already know this news from Samaria; we do not need a merchant to inform us."

The merchant bowed. "Indeed, the king's eyes are like those of an eagle soaring above the plain. But it may have escaped him that . . ." Huram lowered his voice. "I would not dare say this aloud in Samaria, my Lord General, but with you I can be frank. They say that Ahaziah was pushed. Not only that, but they say it was by his mother's orders. However that may be, it is certain that Ahab's younger son, Jehoram, now rules Israel. Or rather, that Queen Jezebel rules from behind the throne."

My face was close to an open place in the screen. An ivory inlay, a woman's head in a window, seemed to stare at me as I stared past her.

"An evil woman, Queen Jezebel," murmured Lady Doronit. "An unnatural mother. My Lord General," she spoke up so her husband could hear, "the girl is here now."

"Let her come out then," said General Naaman.

My heart thumped so hard, I thought I would choke. This was the moment I had hardly dared hope for. Through Huram, my father had found me. In a very short while I would be no longer a slave, but once again my true self — Adara of Ramoth-Gilead, daughter of Calev ben Oved. Stepping out from behind the screen, I knelt before the general.

General Naaman had me stand up and turn around in front of the merchant. "This is indeed the girl," said Huram as I knelt again. He took a leather purse from his belt and poured a small pile of silver pieces onto the bench. I was surprised to see how small the pile was. Had not the slave dealer paid "Goliath" twice as much for me?

"My Lord Husband," said Lady Doronit through the screen, "that is hardly a fair price for such a slave."

"But, my Lord General," Huram said, "consider that my friend Calev ben Oved has fallen upon hard times. The vineyards of Ramoth-Gilead were badly damaged in the battle — er, your glorious victory — the summer before last, and his flocks were raided afterward."

"My Lady Wife," said General Naaman to the screen, "surely you can understand that a man has a right to his own daughter. The fair thing to do is to let this merchant take the girl home to her father."

"My Lord General is not only a mighty warrior of great prowess and valor," said Lady Doronit, "but also a just judge. Yet I wonder how much this father truly longs to have his daughter again, if he is not willing to redeem her at full price."

"Ah, but my Lord General understands the way of the world," said the merchant. "My friend will never receive a bride price for this daughter. No one would marry her now. The priest assured him that he had no obligation to take her back."

My face felt hot, and the inside of my head buzzed. It seemed that Galya's teachings had caught up with me again.

"And yet," Huram went on, "my friend is a man of tender feeling. He wishes to take his daughter back into his house, dishonored as she is. She would be allowed to tend his young children and help the housekeeper."

So my father wanted to ransom me, if he could do it

for half price, and bring me home — as a servant.

"My Lord General." Lady Doronit stepped out from behind the screen while pulling her scarf across her face. "Does my lord not value my wishes above those of an Israelite farmer? It would please me to keep the girl, Adara. Her sweet face is a like a flower in my courtyard, and her voice flows clear and lively like the stream. She whiles away the hours with her stories."

The general shifted in his carved chair. "But a father's rights . . ."

Lady Doronit murmured, "If indeed this merchant has a friend in Ramoth-Gilead who lost a daughter, and if indeed my handmaiden, Adara, is that daughter."

Huram stiffened and replied, "By the dread right arm of the Storm-god, it is as I have said."

The general heaved a sigh, as if he would rather be leading his troops into battle than making judgments. The merchant spoke again, "My lord, why not ask the girl herself who her father is?"

Above her veil Lady Doronit's eyebrows rose. General Naaman also looked surprised, but he nodded and turned to me. "What do you say then, Adara?"

"My lord — " I did not know what I would say until the words came out of my mouth. "I have never seen this merchant before. My father is Avner ben Gideon" — I put together two names from old stories — "of Ashtaroth."

Huram gaped at me. For once, he had nothing to say.

The general rose, frowning. "There you have it, merchant. You are mistaken, and your mission for your friend is in vain. Meanwhile, I have been wasting the afternoon. The troops are assembled at the training field." Lifting a hand in farewell to Lady Doronit, he strode out of the hall.

Huram's beard trembled, but he could not argue with General Naaman. "Perverse! Ungrateful!" he muttered at the bench as he scooped up the silver pieces. I knew that he meant me.

I scrambled to my feet and followed Lady Doronit as she stepped around the screen and headed back to the garden. Settled at her handwork again, her ladyship told her women what had happened. "Imagine, that merchant thought he could cheat General Naaman's wife!" Her eyes sparkled. "Offering only seven pieces of silver for a fine girl like Adara! Adara," she went on to me, "tell again the story of Ruth and her devotion to Naomi."

"Yes, my lady," I said. But I had to pause and collect my thoughts first. My hands trembled, and the thread winding onto my spindle looked lumpier than young Lila's. What had I done? I was not sure I had chosen wisely.

Chapter 17

The Affliction

"What ails the general?" asked Sima, pouring more stew into the common dish. It was suppertime, a few days later. As usual, the women and girl slaves waited on Aharon and the other men and boys. We ate after the men were finished.

"Nothing ails Lord General Naaman — Great Mother Asherah forbid it. Hold your tongue." Raiza glared at Sima and made her usual sign to ward off bad luck.

But the steward paused in the act of scooping stew to his mouth with bread. "Wait — why do you ask, Sima?"

"I do not wish to bring bad luck," said Sima primly. As the steward made an impatient gesture, she went on, "Only that the general's manservant said the general would not let him help him change his tunic."

"No doubt the manservant is out of favor with the general," snapped Raiza.

"In that case, my Lord General would have sent him to eat with the rest of us," Aharon pointed out.

No one knew what to make of this odd bit of information. But now that Sima had brought up the question, I paid more attention when I saw the general the next day. I happened to be in the outer courtyard as he was leaving the house, so I opened the gate for him and his attendants.

Rubbing the backs of his hands and frowning, General Naaman almost failed to notice me. But then he turned toward me and smiled his easy smile. "Adara, little antelope. You have found favor with Lady Doronit, have you not?"

I smiled back. "Her ladyship is kind," I answered. Could his tunic conceal something that he did not want even his manservant to see?

One afternoon the next week, a physician from the palace of King Ben-Hadad arrived at the general's gates. I was attending General Naaman and Lady Doronit in the garden courtyard, fanning cool air at them from the stream. The general lounged on a couch while her ladyship sat beside his head, playing the lyre and chatting about this and that. I tried not to stare at General Naaman, but it did seem there was a bald patch in the beard on his square left jaw.

As her ladyship spoke of the coming harvest festival,

when General Naaman would accompany the king into the temple of Hadad again, Aharon appeared in the doorway. "A visitor at the gate, my Lord General. It is King Ben-Hadad's royal physician."

The general jerked upright, bumping Lady Doronit's hand so that the lyre strings twanged harshly. "I have no need of a physician," he told the steward. "Send him away."

The steward bowed. "As my Lord General wishes," he said, but he did not move from the doorway. "King Ben-Hadad himself (may he live forever) has sent him to treat my Lord General."

"I have no need of a physician! Have you grown deaf?"

Lady Doronit looked alarmed, and she laid a hand on the general's arm. "My Lord, of course you have no need of a physician, and there must be some mistake. But would it not be courteous to the king (may he live forever) to receive the one he has sent?"

The general took a deep breath and shook his head as if to clear it. "Let the physician enter, then."

The physician was an Egyptian. He had no beard, and his wig made his head seem larger than normal, as if it were stuffed with knowledge. His words were polite, but he seemed to say by the way he stood and spoke that he was in charge, not the general. After exchanging greetings, he said, "May I request that the general remove his tunic, so that I may determine his condition and prescribe treatment?"

The general scowled. "You snake of the Nile, how do you dare . . ." But then a worried look — I had never seen General Naaman worried — crossed his face. He pulled his tunic over his head.

Staring at her husband's bare chest, Lady Doronit stifled a gasp. From my position I saw his back, and I drew my breath in sharply, too. The olive-brown skin was marred by patches of deathly white.

The physician did not gasp in horror, but he peered at Naaman from every angle, nodding and muttering, "Mm-hm, mm-hm." Then he had the general put his tunic back on. "This affliction is a serious matter," he announced, "but it can be remedied if my instructions are followed exactly. My Lord General has a condition of the skin. He must be anointed daily with oil of anise, and drink a potion prepared from a syrup of figs mixed with an infusion of wormwood. I will give the directions to a trusted servant."

The general seemed relieved, and so did Lady Doronit. "I will prepare the potion with my own hands," she said.

For the next few days General Naaman followed the royal physician's instructions, and I heard him talking cheerfully to his attendants about preparations for the harvest festival ceremonies. Then one morning, bringing a tray of milk and fruit to Lady Doronit, I heard the crash of pottery breaking in the courtyard.

"That Egyptian quack!" roared General Naaman. He put on a mincing Egyptian accent. "'My Lord General has a condition of the skin.' What wisdom! What discernment! I will force this foul brew down his throat, and see how he likes it. If I catch him outside the palace, I will knock his silly beardless head from his scrawny shoulders!"

I glimpsed a shattered goblet on the stones of the courtyard, and then I jumped aside as the general stomped through the doorway. More of his beard had fallen out, and a patch of the ugly white had appeared under one eye.

During the days leading up to the harvest festival, General Naaman tried one remedy after the other. A magician came and chanted a spell to banish the demon that must be causing this affliction. A herbalist was summoned, and he burned herbs in the braziers in every room, to purify the air. A sculptor of great skill made a clay figure of the general, which was then painted skin-brown and glazed perfectly smooth.

Meanwhile, the white blotches spread over General Naaman's skin like mold on a rotten melon. I wished holy Elisha were here in Damascus instead of far away in Samaria. Sometimes I caught myself imagining that the holy man appeared at the general's gate. But that seemed too much like my old daydream of my father rescuing me. I felt there was something I ought to do, but I did not know what.

By the day of the harvest festival, General Naaman was wearing a cloak over his head and arms, in spite of the late-summer heat. No escort came from the king to summon the general to the palace, from which he and the king were to process to the temple.

In the slaves' quarters, there was no roasted kid for our harvest feast. One of the litter-bearers grumbled over the lentil stew, and Raiza snapped at him. "If the master cannot rejoice, why should the slaves feast? You will be a lucky slave if lentil stew is the worst thing that happens to you."

Raiza carried a small dish of lentils to the shrine outside the kitchen. The slaves looked at each other with fear in their eyes.

Chapter 18

Demand for a Sacrifice

The morning after that gloomy harvest festival, I brought Lady Doronit a tray of bread and apricots. She was sitting on her couch with her brow puckered. "Adara, go fetch the old woman who tells fortunes in the market."

This was the same fortune-teller of Raiza's who had visited Lady Doronit before. Today Lady Doronit did not banter with the fortune-teller, and the old woman seemed to understand her mood. Silently she sprinkled her powders on the coals of a brazier. As a greenish smoke swirled up, she stared into the haze and made motions with her hands. "My lady is troubled over the affliction of one close to her," she said. "A blight has fallen upon him, and he has lost favor in high places."

That was not a great feat of fortune-telling, I

thought. By now everyone in Damascus knew that General Naaman's skin was moldy white and his beard and hair were falling out. And that King Ben-Hadad no longer allowed his favorite General to accompany him into the temple of Hadad.

Still gazing into the smoke, the old woman made a hissing noise through the gaps in her front teeth. "What do you see?" urged Lady Doronit.

"I see . . . I see a long journey for my Lord General. My lady goes with him, and a girl" — she glanced at me — "yes, this handmaiden. But the journey is a bitter disappointment." The fortune-teller looked sincerely puzzled. "No, wait! The journey is a great success. Or perhaps — "

"Which is it, you miserable hag?" exclaimed Lady Doronit.

"A success, for sure, my lady. Oh, yes, a success!" The woman held out her hand. "My powders are costly."

Lady Doronit looked mistrustful, but she gave the woman a piece of silver and had me take her to the kitchen for a meal. Later that day I heard Lady Doronit say to Raiza, "I think the fortune teller could have made up a better story. A journey! My lord is not a trader. He might lead the army to do battle, but then I would not go with him. And why would she say that Adara will go?"

I had wondered that, too. Whether a particular slave went on the journey or not — surely that was not important enough to mention, in foretelling the future. That was like saying, "You will go on a journey, and that camel will carry your baggage."

★ ★ ★

Weeks went by. The general went out less and less, even wrapped in his cloak. He no longer ordered his chariot and sent word to his officers to hunt lions in the desert with him. At last he would not even visit the army's drill ground to observe the training.

They said in the slaves' quarters that the general had shouted at his sons and driven them out of his sight. The boys had only asked when he would take them to see the soldiers drill, as he had promised. "Never!" he had roared. "Go back to your nursemaids." Maimon, the older boy, was especially hurt by this, since he was much too old for a nursemaid.

General Naaman spent much time slumped on a bench in his courtyard, a wine cup in his hand. He called Lady Doronit to keep him company, but then he found fault with everything she did. "Your lyre is out of tune," he complained. Or, "Why do you not smile?" Or, "Why do you smile, when there is nothing to smile about? Why do you not give me more sons?"

Or, worse, the general would sit silently with his cloak pulled over his head. From time to time he would lift the goblet into the shadow of the cloak. Whatever my lady said, he answered with a grunt.

Once I was in the courtyard, watering the garden, as

Aharon bent to refill the general's wine cup. "My Lord General," said the steward in a low voice, "would it not be well for us to ride out of the city and inspect your fields and flocks? I am concerned — "

"Do not concern yourself," said the general. "King Ben-Hadad gave me those fields and flocks when he was pleased with me. Soon he will take them back, and someone else will have to inspect them."

Those are the words of a man without hope, I thought. He would have hope, if he knew what a great healer the holy man Elisha was. But who was I to tell him? Why would he believe me, when he was not a worshipper of Elisha's God, Yahweh? No, the general would only fly into a rage if I tried to give him hope.

One morning when the sun was just above the rooftops, a richly decorated litter arrived at General Naaman's gate. "Behold, the high priest of Hadad," announced one of the guards attending the litter. He gestured toward an old man, richly dressed, wearing a necklace of golden calves.

The steward bowed low, and so did the rest of us in the courtyard. "Your master honors my master," said Aharon to the high priest's servant, in his most formal manner. He led the way toward the reception hall.

Sima and I exchanged looks. The general had taken to sleeping late, and he had not changed his tunic in days. The high priest was in for a wait.

One of the temple litter-bearers cast a pitying look around the courtyard. "This household is cursed. Your master must have offended the gods."

Raiza made her sign against bad luck, but listlessly, as if she thought it was too late. "How so?" she protested. "The Lord General observes the feast days. He bows to the household gods when he enters our gates. They say he gives Hadad the victory, every battle he wins."

The high priest's man shrugged. "The gods are not reasonable. Maybe they are angry because the general is so favored. He is handsome, a mighty warrior, beloved of the king, adored by his soldiers, blessed with sons. Maybe the gods want him to make a special sacrifice."

"The Lord General has made special sacrifices," said Raiza indignantly. "For the harvest festival he sent to the temple of Hadad a hundred white bullocks, each without blemish."

The high priest's man half-closed his eyes in a knowing way. "Obviously, that was not the right sacrifice to satisfy the gods. This curse must be removed, and soon, before it spreads and blights the rest of Damascus."

The other litter bearers began suggesting ways that General Naaman might placate the gods. He might slash a scar in his face, or even cut off one of his fingers. I could not stand to listen to the high priest's men, so I left to make my rounds of filling the household lamps.

I did not see the high priest leave, but I noticed about midmorning that his litter and guards were gone from the outer courtyard. The next moment, there was a terrible shriek from the family's chambers.

"My lady!" exclaimed Raiza. She dashed off, heedless of her rheumatism. I ran after her.

We found Lady Doronit in the nursery. She was clutching her older son against her, so hard that he was protesting and struggling to get away. The nursemaids were crying out loud, but Lady Doronit's screams rose above the din: "No! No! Not Maimon! No!"

"Great Mother Asherah," whimpered Raiza. "Surely the king will not allow it, not in civilized Damascus."

At first I did not understand what she meant, although I was sure it must be a horror to make my blood run cold. Then I remembered a story I had once heard — and tried to forget. It told of a king who sacrificed his own son on the city walls to buy the protection of the gods.

This must be what the high priest had told General Naaman, and the general had told his wife. The gods demanded a special sacrifice before they took away his affliction. They demanded a son.

"No!" My cry joined the screams of Lady Doronit and the other women. We all huddled around Lady Doronit, as if that could be any protection. I wished with all my heart that B'rinna were here.

B'rinna could comfort her ladyship by explaining the way she understood her God. She did not believe that Yahweh sent afflictions. When the famine struck Samaria and she had nothing to eat and her sons were about to be sold into slavery, her neighbors had said she must have sinned. God was punishing her.

But holy Elisha had denied that. God was merciful, he had told B'rinna. God wanted to help her.

That night, as I drifted off to sleep, Sima and one of the other girls were still talking about the High Priest's visit in horrified whispers. But their voices seemed far away, as if I were not really in Damascus. I comforted myself by imagining B'rinna. I felt her arms around me, and the scent of coriander in her robe. I also imagined holy Elisha with his deep, kind gaze. The two of them somehow mixed together into a figure of loving care.

Then an image of the general came into my mind. It was so startling that I woke right up. This was General Naaman as I had never seen him — on his knees, without his fine clothes and armor, bare-headed. And Elisha held out his hands to the Aramean general with the same tenderness he had shown to the widow B'rinna.

Chapter 19

Good News

Naaman crouched in his chamber by himself. He had hardly slept at all the night before, after the high priest's visit. He was not on his ivory-inlaid bed, but in a corner on the hard floor. That seemed more fitting. Truly the gods hate me, he thought.

He heard footsteps outside the door, and voices, but he did not get up. He had ordered his manservant to let no one in.

And yet the curtain was pushed aside.

"I do not wish to be disturbed," growled Naaman. It made him angry that he even had to speak.

Still, Doronit entered. She looked timid but determined. "Good morning, my husband."

Scowling, Naaman opened his mouth to tell her to go away. But then he noticed how different she looked than when he had last seen her yesterday. Yesterday, she had flung herself around screaming, her hair loose and wild, her eye paint smeared under her reddened eyes. Now she looked neat and calm, although tired. She had brought a slave with her — Adara.

Kneeling beside Naaman, Doronit took his hands. He flinched and tried to pull them away, to hide their hideous white-blotched skin from her sight. "Naaman, my love!" Doronit's face was glowing. "I have such good news. There is a holy man in Samaria who could cure you."

He stared at her, wondering if her grief had driven her mad. "A holy — in Samaria, the enemy's capital?" He gave a short laugh. "Where did you hear this?"

"Adara told me," said Doronit.

Naaman laughed again, a harsh cackle. "I see. A slave girl told you. So you have it on the best authority."

"Please, my husband. Let her speak."

The girl was kneeling beside Doronit, waiting with her head bowed and hands together for his permission. Naaman felt that he should stay angry, very angry, in order to ward off such a false hope. It must be false, just like the hope raised by the royal physician and all the other quacks. Still, he did not have the strength to be angry. He grunted permission.

Adara raised her eyes to his and began, "My Lord General — "

"How do you know a holy man of Samaria?" Naaman interrupted. He was afraid to let her speak, at the same time that he longed to believe her. "You are from Ramoth-Gilead."

"Yes, my Lord," said Adara. "I heard of holy Elisha from our housekeeper, before I was captured and brought to Damascus. I have not seen him in the flesh, but I know him through his powerful spirit."

Naaman grunted again. "Even if there is such a man in Samaria who could cure me" — in spite of himself, his heart beat faster as he said the words — "why would a holy man of Israel want to cure the commander of the army of Aram?"

The girl almost smiled. Her expression seemed to say that she too thought it was absurd but wonderfully true. She gazed at him with calm tenderness, as if she were the mighty general and he were the humble slave. "I know he would, my lord."

Naaman felt his eyes sting, and he realized with horror that he was going to cry. He leapt to his feet, flailing his arms. "Out! Out, both of you foolish women!"

Scrambling out of his reach, Doronit and the girl ducked under the door curtain. Not a moment too soon, before the mighty commander of the armies of Aram burst into spasms of sobs.

Chapter 20

To Samaria

When the general chased us out of his chamber, I was afraid that Lady Doronit and I had failed. He was making dreadful choked noises as we escaped down the corridor. But her ladyship halted, let out a long breath, and hugged me. I could feel her whole body shaking. "He will make the journey to Samaria," she said. "He will ask the king's permission to go, this very day."

Sure enough, General Naaman visited the palace that afternoon and returned with a scroll sealed with the great seal of Aram. King Ben-Hadad had given the journey his blessing. The scroll was an official letter from Ben-Hadad to King Jehoram of Israel, explaining why the king of Aram was sending the commander of his armies to Samaria.

For the next two days the whole household worked

early and late, gathering supplies and equipment and packing them. The following morning, General Naaman's chariot led his caravan out the north gate of Damascus. He did not ride his war chariot, of course, for he went to Israel in peace. When we reached the foothills, all the chariots would have to be taken apart and loaded onto camels, since they could not be driven over the rough mountain trails. They would be put together again outside Samaria, so that the general could enter the city in the manner befitting his rank.

Besides General Naaman's chariots and the chariots of his officers and of Lady Doronit, the caravan included a string of camels and donkeys. Some of the pack animals were laden with gifts for the holy man: ten talents of silver, six thousand shekels of gold, and ten costly kilts and robes to wear on feast days. Then there were the necessary soldiers to protect the caravan from bandits, and the necessary attendants.

To my surprise, I was one of the attendants traveling to Samaria. "Why, it must all come about as the fortune-teller predicted," said Lady Doronit. In a merry mood these days, she liked the joke that she would make the fortune-teller's prediction come true.

Lady Doronit did not explain her real reason for taking me, but Raiza thought it was clear. "You, Adara, are the one who understands the Israelite magician. The general may need your help when he reaches Samaria."

"Elisha is a holy man, not a magician," I said, but I knew Raiza did not see any difference.

Sima gave a knowing sniff. "The general is taking Lady Doronit so that he can blame her, if the holy man does not cure him. And Lady Doronit is taking Adara so that she can blame her, if this cure fails." I thought perhaps Sima was right, but I also thought she wished she were traveling to Samaria. There was a wistful look in her eyes as I waved good-bye, following her ladyship's chariot out the courtyard gate.

We traveled the King's Way from Damascus to Ramoth-Gilead, the reverse of the journey I had made two years ago. It was again the dry season, but every scene we passed through looked different to me. Of course I was much more comfortable, for I rode a donkey, and I was not thinking about the blisters on my feet. But the main difference was that now I was not trying to push the wheel of time back. I was trying to roll it forward to Samaria, to the moment when General Naaman stood before Elisha and was healed.

The general was pushing forward, too. He still kept himself covered with his cloak, but I caught glimpses of his face now and then, and he was almost smiling. He seemed impatient each time the caravan stopped to rest, but he urged us on with a cheerful voice.

Every once in a while I realized that all the hopes of this journey depended on my word alone. Then I would go cold with fear. Who was I to send an entire caravan — the commander of the armies of Aram, his wife and attendants and companions, and a train of costly gifts — all the way from Damascus to Samaria?

But then I would think of how I felt the presence of holy Elisha, how he cared for me, a miserable slave girl in a faraway city. It was on Elisha, not on me, that General Naaman's hopes depended. Surely the holy man would have pity on a mighty general, traveling so far over mountains and plains and rivers to seek his help.

Late in the afternoon of the fourth day, we passed Ramoth-Gilead without pausing. The town seemed smaller than I had remembered. I wondered if my family was in the vineyards, picking grapes. I could not see Father's vineyard from the road, but I thought I glimpsed the top of his watchtower.

I imagined B'rinna in the rows of vines, keeping an eye on Lila as she piled bunches of grapes in a two-handled basket. I wished I could stop and let her know that I was well, and tell her where I was going with General Naaman. "And all because of you, because you told me about holy Elisha, B'rinna!" I smiled at the thought of her eyes opening in amazement, her hands pressed over her mouth.

Then it crossed my mind that all this was happening also because I had sneaked off to the underground well on the day of the battle. If I had not been captured and taken to Damascus and enslaved, I would not have been able to tell Lady Doronit about Elisha. Was it then a good thing that I had been so disobedient and foolish? Or could the Lord God Yahweh turn a mistake into a miracle?

The next day we left the King's Way at the town of Mahanaim, on the Jabbok River. The general's train followed the river west, down from the high plain of Gilead through the clay bluffs to the Jordan River. On the river bottom the road wound through a tangle of tamarisk and poplar. The air was hot and thick, and the caravan had to stop more often to let the pack animals rest.

As we crossed the Jordan River at a ford, Lady Doronit leaned down from her horse and sniffed. "So this is the Jordan — such an ugly little river compared to our beautiful pure Barada, is it not? Nothing but a muddy trickle."

On the west side of the Jordan the caravan found the mouth of the Farah River. We journeyed up the Farah to the town of Tirzah, in highlands that reminded me of Gilead. The following day, we came upon the royal city of Samaria.

Set on a hill in the middle of rich farmland, Samaria was four times as large as Ramoth-Gilead and ten times as grand. Its stone walls loomed like the bluffs of the Jordan River. If Ramoth-Gilead looked like a headdress, Samaria was like a king's crown.

General Naaman pitched his tents outside the gates and sent a messenger to the palace, requesting an audience with the king of Israel. I waited on Lady Doronit, laying out the robe and jewelry she would wear in the procession the next day. I watched the general's attendants unpack the pieces of his chariot and ready it for his entrance into the city.

The next morning, General Naaman rode under the massive watchtowers and into Samaria. Between the outer wall and the inner wall was a marketplace, where people crowded to see the commander of the armies of Aram. I noticed they stayed back a certain distance, though. I heard a father say to the little son on his shoulder, "There, see how Yahweh has cursed the enemy of Israel. God has turned his flesh white and unclean."

From the market we passed through a second gate into the city itself. All along our route, Samaritans watched the procession from their rooftops. I quickly got tired of craning my neck to look up at them, and besides, the sun above the housetops was blinding. But something made me glance up once more as we passed a certain house. It was an ordinary mud-brick house in a humble section of the city.

On that rooftop, leaning on a staff, stood a man with long, untrimmed hair and beard. I could not make out the features of his face, for the sun blazed directly behind him. But I knew who he was.

Chapter 21

An Audience with the King of Israel

"It is holy Elisha!" I cried out. "My lady!" Lady Doronit's chariot was in front of me. "Tell them to stop. There is the prophet himself!"

Lady Doronit tried to look where I was pointing, but the sun blinded her. "Never mind, Adara. The general must call on King Jehoram first. It is a necessary courtesy."

I knew nothing of the proper etiquette between nations. As the procession wound upward through the city, I was silent. But I had a strong feeling that we were going in the wrong direction.

At the very crown of the hill we came to a ring of yet more walls and guard towers. This was the palace of King Jehoram of Israel, second son of the dead King Ahab.

At the entrance of the palace General Naaman dismounted from his chariot. Lady Doronit drew her veil across her face — careful not to cover her gold necklace and bracelets — and stepped down from her chariot, too. I left my donkey and followed the rest of the procession between the two enormous gold statues guarding the palace doors. The statues were cherubim, creatures with a man's head, the body of a lion, and wings like a great swooping eagle's. The precious stones in their eyes seemed to watch as we walked past.

I had not seen the palace of King Ben-Hadad in Damascus, but I could not imagine that it could be any grander than this. I stared around at the brightly painted panels on the walls, the pillars crowned with rows of gold-leaf pomegranates, the inlaid ivory carved with palm trees and flowers.

At the door of the audience hall, General Naaman's officers and guards were asked to lay down their spears. The Arameans did not like this, but at a gesture from the general they stacked their weapons against the wall, and we entered the grand hall. At the far end, broad steps led to a platform with two thrones. Golden lions stood at the ends of each step, and golden lions held up the armrests of each throne. On one throne, a man in purple robes waited.

On the other throne sat a woman. As we came closer, I could see gold threads shining in the cloth of her robes. She seemed to be somewhat older than Lady Doronit, as far as I could tell through the paint on her face. I caught my breath. This must be Queen Jezebel — the woman who could do anything she wanted.

Stopping in front of the platform, General Naaman bowed low enough for politeness. "I, Naaman, bring greetings to His Majesty King Jehoram of Israel from King Ben-Hadad of Aram. Behold, a letter to King Jehoram from King Ben-Hadad."

An Israelite minister stepped forward to accept the scroll and present it to the king. I noticed that the king looked very young, perhaps not as old as my half brother, Dov. Breaking the seal, King Jehoram handed the letter to a scribe. The scribe read aloud:

"From His Majesty Ben-Hadad of Aram, to His Majesty Jehoram ben Ahab of Israel, greetings. I have sent to you my servant Naaman, commanding general of the armies of Aram, victor of the battle of Ramoth-Gilead. Know that he comes to Samaria in peace, that you may cure him of his unclean disease."

My heart sank. King Ben-Hadad's scribe had gotten it wrong. "But this is not right!" I whispered to Lady Doronit. "It is the holy man, not the king, who can cure."

Lady Doronit looked worried. "That boy-king clearly could not cure a pimple, for he still has some."

Others must have thought the same thing, for murmurs broke out up and down the hall. Queen Mother Jezebel exclaimed, "Surely this is a cowardly excuse for war! Was it not enough to slay my husband at the battle of Ramoth-Gilead? Will Ben-Hadad now march on Samaria if his commander is not cured?"

Jumping to his feet, King Jehoram tore a long rip in his purple robe. "Woe to the throne of Israel! Am I Baal or Yahweh, to cure a man of his unclean disease?" He stared around at his ministers. "Do you see how the King of Aram is picking a fight with me?"

The hall filled with excited babble. General Naaman shouted, "Not so, Your Majesty — why would I think you could cure me? There has been a mistake! King Ben-Hadad must have meant that you should order the holy man to cure me."

But it was too noisy for General Naaman's words to reach the king. Besides, the king was not listening to anyone except the Queen Mother. Gripping his arm, she was speaking urgently into his ear and gesturing around the hall. I looked at the royal guards standing ready with their spears and thought, General Naaman and his men are unarmed.

Then there was a new commotion at the rear of the hall. One of the royal guards pushed his way forward to the foot of the steps and bowed to King Jehoram. The queen motioned an attendant to strike a gong. In the silence that followed, the guard announced, "Elisha, prophet of Yahweh, bids General Naaman to come to him."

The queen's furrowed brow smoothed out — in fact, she smiled. She said to her son, "What a fine solution, Your Majesty. Let the prophet deal with the general."

"Yes, yes," said Jehoram. "This is a matter for a holy

man. Let all present bear witness that I do my utmost to fulfill His Majesty of Aram's request, in sending Commanding General Naaman to Elisha." His voice cracked with relief. "The audience is finished."

"What an incompetent fool," said General Naaman to his officers, not bothering to keep his voice down. "His father, Ahab, was ten times the man."

As we began to file out of the hall, one of the officers remarked, "So is his mother." They laughed. The Israelite guards scowled, but they let us pass.

One of the royal guards, the man who had brought Elisha's message, led General Naaman's train out of the palace and through the city. Back in the modest neighborhood where I had glimpsed the holy man, the guard stopped in front of the same mud-brick house. "Behold, the dwelling of Elisha."

General Naaman looked surprised, but he nodded to one of his officers. The officer walked up to the door and raised his fist to knock. Just then, a man in a plain tunic stepped out and bowed to the general.

"Can this squinty-eyed fellow be the great healer?" murmured Lady Doronit.

"Greetings to Commander Naaman from my master, holy Elisha," said the man. "The prophet of Yahweh knows what you desire. He bids you go to the Jordan River and wash seven times. Then, says my master, your flesh will be restored. You will be healed, and you will be clean."

Chapter 22

The Muddy Trickle

For a moment, no one spoke. Then the officer near the door shouted, "Where are your manners, you flea-bitten Israelite dog? The holy man himself must appear to the Lord General, not send him a message through a servant."

The servant cringed, but he repeated, "Thus says my master to Naaman of Damascus: Go to the Jordan River and wash seven times, and you will be whole." As the officer lunged at him, he ducked back into the house, slammed the door, and barred it.

Next to me, Lady Doronit moaned. I was too shocked to make a noise or even move.

General Naaman brought his fist down on the rail of his chariot. "Is that all?" His cloak fell back from his mangy hair, showing his face reddened in between the blotches of white. "Is this what I journeyed all the way from Damascus for? The holy man does not even greet me himself? He does not lift his arms to the sky and call upon his God, Yahweh? He does not wave his hands over me like a proper healer and cure my disease?"

Someone must do something, I thought. After being treated this way, General Naaman would never do what Elisha said. He would not be cured. Someone . . . I looked all around at the people waiting in the street. The officers and guards, the general's attendants, Lady Doronit, the camel drivers — none of them could help.

All their eyes were fixed on General Naaman as he ranted on. "'Go wash in the Jordan River,' he says! The Jordan, that muddy trickle! Why could I not remain in Damascus and wash in the sweet clear water there?"

No one saw me slip off my donkey and sneak into the alley. I must speak with holy Elisha and explain to him, I thought. A brick missing from the courtyard wall gave me a toehold, and I boosted myself up and over.

I landed in the small courtyard in front of the man I had glimpsed earlier. He sat on a bench as if he was waiting for me, for he did not seem surprised to see a girl climbing over his wall. Now that I could see him plainly, he looked just as I had imagined him — just as B'rinna had described Elisha, except that this man's beard was gray. He wore a mantle of goatskin, and he had a deep, quiet gaze.

"Oh, please, sir!" I dropped onto my knees. "Please go speak with my master yourself. I am afraid he will not do as your servant told him. He is so insulted! Could you not speak kindly to him, as you did once to B'rinna?"

"Ah, B'rinna." Elisha smiled at the memory, but then he shook his head. "The poor widow B'rinna needed only kindness in order to receive the Lord God's mercy. But the mighty General Naaman needs to humble himself first."

"But what if he will not humble himself?" I pleaded. "Could you not explain it to him, at least? He does not understand — " My voice trailed off, and I looked away from the holy man's deep-set, calm eyes.

"If Naaman will not humble himself," he said sadly, "he will not be healed." I began to plead again, but he held up his hand. "Enough. It is not up to me, now, and it is not up to you, my daughter. You have done your part, Adara of Ramoth-Gilead." He stood up, smiling again. "Come, let me boost you back over the wall."

★   ★   ★

It was a wretched journey from Samaria to Tirzah and from Tirzah back down the Farah River to the Jordan. All of us tried to stay away from the general, whether he was raging out loud or sunk in a black silence. I would have stayed away from Lady Doronit, too, except that she called me to her side.

"Why did not the holy man greet the general?" she

wailed. "Did he not understand that this was Naaman, commander of the armies of Aram, Mighty Thunderbolt of Hadad?" Not waiting for me to answer, "Why did you tell me that Elisha would cure my husband? Why did I believe you? It was an evil day when I found you in the slave market. Get out of my sight — go!"

I was glad to turn my donkey back to the end of the train. But later that day, she summoned me again. "How do we know the holy man was even at home? Perhaps his servant made up that insulting message."

Hesitantly, I told her ladyship I had spoken to the prophet himself. "He said the general must become . . . humble."

Jerking her horse around to block the trail, Lady Doronit fixed me with a stare. "When we return to Damascus, you will discover what 'humble' means. Now, get out of my sight!"

As we rode across the river bottom, I felt something pressing me, heavier and heavier — something more than the hot, thick air. It reminded me of the way I had felt two years ago, crouching in the cave and watching the end of the battle of Ramoth-Gilead. Now, as General Naaman rode up to the river's edge without slowing, my feeling was unbearable.

Beating my heels against my donkey's sides, I pushed my way to the general's side. "My Lord General! Here is the Jordan River. Would it not be easy to do as the holy man said?"

General Naaman did not bother to answer me. But to my surprise, Lady Doronit rode up on the General's other side and added her pleas. "My husband! I beg you. If the holy man had told you to do some mighty feat, such as running all the way up Mount Hermon, would you not have done it? Here we are at the Jordan. It would take only a little while to wash. Why not try it?"

"You want me to wash in that?" The general pointed to the sluggish brown stream in front of his horse. "I would not have my camels washed in it." He turned and stared at his wife. "This was your evil idea. A woman should not presume to tell her husband what to do, and her husband should not heed her. Listen to Adara, you told me. Adara of the sweet face! If this dried-up gutter Jordan had more water in it, I would drown the stupid brat."

"Lord General, with all respect — " Now that we were actually at the Jordan River, General Naaman's companions seemed to feel the urgency as I did. They crowded around the general, pleading with him to try the cure.

"Silence!" roared the general. He pulled his cloak over his head and urged his horse forward, scattering the officers and splashing mud onto Lady Doronit's robe.

I waited for the rest of the procession to go by before I let my donkey follow the last camel across the ford. The Jordan River, General Naaman's one chance for healing, was now behind us. I was as grieved as if B'rinna herself had deceived me. What good is healing, I reproached her in my mind, if it is offered in such a way that he refuses it?

By the time we reached the foot of the bluffs on the east bank, I was sunk in gloom. It took me a moment to realize the procession had stopped. I wondered why we were halting here, when it was not yet near evening. Then I saw the general riding back down the line. There was a strange calm on his face as he brushed past us. "Wait here," he muttered to no one in particular. We watched the general disappear in the direction of the Jordan River.

Chapter 23

Clean

As Naaman rode toward the river, a sense started to grow on him that he ought to dismount. He swung off his horse, tied it to a palm tree, and continued on foot. Then it came to him that he should not be wearing shoes. He pulled off his boots, left them beside the path, and went on barefoot.

A few steps farther, it seemed to Naaman that the cloak over his head was getting in the way. He let it fall back on his shoulders, then tossed it aside. There was no one here to see him, after all.

In the steamy air of the river bottom, it seemed foolish to wear a kilt over his tunic. He untied his belt, unwound the kilt, and left them both on a boulder. On second thought, he turned back, pulled off his bronze armbands, and set them on top of the kilt.

Naaman stood at the edge of the Jordan River, where the water barely flowed from one pool to the next. He did not feel like the commander of the armies of Aram, Thunderbolt of the Right Hand of Hadad. The river gorge around him was huge and the sky above even more vast. He felt small and alone. Somehow it was not a bad feeling. It was simply true.

"Naaman."

"Here I am, Lord," said Naaman, as if he were a servant.

"Naaman."

"Here I am, Lord."

"Naaman."

With a long sigh, Naaman pulled his tunic over his head. He saw the white blotches that were his skin, but somehow the horror was gone. The river gorge did not shrink back in disgust from the sight of him. The sky did not hide its eye, the sun.

The deepest pool was so shallow that he had to lie down in it to get himself wet. Rising, he wiped his face and watched the brown water run down his arms and legs.

Seven times.

Again and again Naaman stretched out in the muddy pool and dunked his head. Suddenly it struck him how he must look, wallowing like a hippopotamus. He began to laugh. Good riddance to that dignified fool, the mighty hero Naaman! "Behold — Naaman, the Clean!" He stretched his arms to the sky.

"Thank you, Lord!"

As he walked back up the path, gathering his clothes and putting them on, Naaman could not stop laughing. It made no sense. He had washed himself in the Jordan River, and now he was healed. It was absurd. But he was healed! More than healed — he felt new from the inside out.

Everything around Naaman looked new. How beautiful the riverbed was, set among the cliffs! How beautiful the trail that followed the Jabbok River eastward! Doronit and his officers were waiting. At the thought of his wife and friends, his heart overflowed. They had loved him so faithfully, hideous and unlovable though he had been.

Swinging onto his horse, Naaman galloped up the path to where the others waited. "I am clean! Clean! The God of Elisha has healed me!"

They stared at him with anxious faces. Naaman glanced down at his arms and legs, gray with drying mud. The mud must also be caked in his hair and beard. He laughed. "Under the mud, I am clean. Rejoice with me!"

"My Lord General," said Doronit in a trembling voice. "Will you rest in the shade for a while before we go on?"

She thought he had gone mad under the strain. Naaman looked around the group. They all thought he was mad — all except the slave girl, Adara, whose face was shining.

Chapter 24

Adara's Wish

General Naaman was not gone long, but Lady Doronit fretted the whole time. She begged his officers to follow him and make sure he was not going to kill himself. The officers were worried, too, but they did not want to disobey the general's order to wait for him.

Finally the general's favorite officer rode down the trail a little way. He returned looking relieved. He had found General Naaman's horse with the sword hanging from the saddle. "If the Lord General meant to harm himself, surely he would have taken his sword."

I never doubted that the general was going to wash himself in the Jordan River, as Elisha had told him to do. But it was hard for me to wait, too. I turned my donkey loose to graze, sat down on a boulder, and sang to myself,

Let the righteous be merry and joyful!
For he delivers the needy when he calls,
the poor and him who has no helper.

And then, with a thunder of hoofbeats, General Naaman galloped up to us. "I am clean! Clean!" He leaped off his horse and embraced Lady Doronit, then each of his officers, leaving streaks of mud on their clothes.

They clearly thought he was crazed, but that did not seem to trouble the general. He beamed at them and shrugged. "You will see, in time." His glance fell on me, and he beamed all the more. "Adara, at least, knows I am healed."

Now the general was eager to return to Samaria to thank Elisha and present the gifts to him. The journey seemed much shorter than the way we had just come, even though much of the road was uphill. General Naaman was overcome with joy at every least thing. I heard him exclaim to an officer, "Is the sky not blue, bluer than it has ever been? See how it grows yet bluer as we climb into the hills?" And later, to Lady Doronit, "The dry grass on the hills, is it not golden? From a distance it looks like the fur of a lioness, does it not? You could almost reach out and stroke it."

At first the others merely agreed with everything General Naaman said. I saw them sneak glances at his hands, and at the bare calves of his legs. Little by little the mud flaked off, revealing smooth olive-brown skin.

Gradually they seemed to believe that he was not mad — only astonished with happiness.

In the city of Samaria again, General Naaman's procession halted in front of Elisha's mud-brick house. The general jumped down from his chariot. Again, before he could knock, Elisha's door opened. This time, the holy man himself stepped out.

"Behold," exclaimed General Naaman, stretching his arms out to show himself. "Now I know that there is no God in all the world, except in Israel." He gestured at the string of camels behind him. "Please accept these gifts from your servant."

Elisha's face broke into a broad smile. "Rejoice before God, praise his name!" He laughed out loud, and General Naaman laughed, too, as if they shared a joke. Then Elisha calmed himself and added formally, "As the Lord lives, whom I serve, I will not take anything."

The Aramean commander looked amazed. "But I brought these gifts all the way from Damascus for you: ten talents of silver, six thousand shekels of gold, and ten festal garments. Must I carry them all the way back? I beg you, do me the favor of accepting them."

Elisha shook his head. General Naaman urged him again and again, but each time the holy man refused calmly. I thought, the holy man is waiting to speak of something else.

Finally General Naaman seemed to realize that himself, and he stopped arguing. Elisha asked, "Now that you are healed, Naaman of Damascus, how will you live?"

"I have been thinking that I should return to Damascus and worship the Lord God Yahweh there," said General Naaman. Elisha nodded, and General Naaman went on, "I will need to take some earth from Samaria, as much as two mules can carry, to make a foundation for a shrine to Yahweh in Damascus. For naturally God must be worshiped on his own soil."

Elisha raised an amused eyebrow, but he said, "Naturally."

"And also — " General Naaman hesitated, looking troubled. "Once I am back in Damascus, healed, King Ben-Hadad will expect me to accompany him into the temple of Hadad and take part in the rituals. Will your God allow me? Will he understand that in truth I worship only him?"

Once more Elisha nodded. He gazed into Naaman's eyes with a look that seemed to speak from deep inside the holy man to deep inside the general. "*Shalom,* peace."

• • •

On the journey back to the King's Way, General Naaman seemed as happy as a groom on his wedding day. He was especially tender with Lady Doronit, often riding beside her and reaching out to touch her hand. As for my lady, she had eyes only for her husband. The two of them acted the way Hannah used to say she and

Dov had acted, when they were first married.

As we followed the Jabbok River up through the bluffs on the east side of the Jordan, Lady Doronit called me to her side. "My Lord General and I are grateful to you, Adara, for leading him to the healer of Israel. Ask for whatever you wish, and it will be given to you." She swallowed after she said this, as if she feared I might ask too much.

"I wish to be free," I said.

"Of course you are no longer a slave!" exclaimed General Naaman, who was riding in front of us. "That goes without saying. Furthermore, Adara, I will give you the greatest reward I can bestow. I will betroth my older son, Maimon, to you."

Lady Doronit made a choking noise. Controlling herself, she said, "My Lord General is the soul of generosity, and he always knows best. But would Adara not rather marry a grown man?"

I was imagining myself betrothed to that little boy who put bugs down my back, and I felt just as horrified as my lady looked. "My Lord General is indeed generous," I said. "But I am not sure I wish to marry at all." The longings I had felt before my capture came rushing up, like an underground spring. "Oh, my Lord General, let me live in your household, only not as a slave. And let me study with a teacher until I can read and write as well as a scribe. And let me one day travel as far as Babylon, and Egypt, and the shores of the Great Sea!"

"This is truly what you wish?" The general looked astonished, then relieved. "Well, then, how else can I reward you? Will you accept the treasure we brought to give the healer?" He gestured at the pack animals, still laden with the silver and gold and costly garments. "You may have it all."

I shook my head. "If holy Elisha would not take it, I should not, either. The only other thing I wish — " B'rinna's dear wrinkled face came into my mind, and my throat hurt so that I could hardly speak. "I wish to bring my foster mother from Ramoth-Gilead back to Damascus."

General Naaman and Lady Doronit gladly agreed. So when the general's train reached the hills above Ramoth-Gilead, I walked down from the road to the vineyards. I took with me a bag of silver, for Lady Doronit urged me to bring at least as much as the bride price my father would have gotten for me.

"A gift makes for a welcome guest," she said.

Chapter 25

The Way Home

I walked over the ridge and down a path toward the terraced vineyards. I was glad for the landmark of my father's watchtower, for his vineyard had looked quite different the last time I picked grapes there. Now there were big gaps in the rows. New vines had been planted where the Aramean army had trampled and burned the old ones, but the little vines were barely noticeable. They would not start to bear fruit for another year or so.

The first person I came to was a girl of about five. I almost passed her by without noticing her, because she was sitting under a vine. She held a half-eaten bunch of grapes, and the front of her tunic was stained purple.

At first I did not recognize her. Then I cried, "Lila, little sister!" I stooped and held out my arms.

"You are so big now."

Lila's eyes grew larger and rounder. She did not answer me or move toward me. "Auntie!" she called over her shoulder. "A strange lady is here."

"Lila! I am Adara." I pulled off my headscarf. "Do you not know me?"

"Adara?" Hannah's mild face appeared at the end of the row. Carrying a young child on her hip, she hurried toward us. "Adara! Great Mother!" She said to Lila, "Go tell *Imma*, Adara is back." She went on as she hugged me, "Husband's sister, we thought you had drowned in the well! Whatever happened to you?"

"What happened to me?" Why did she not know? "Did not the shepherd Ezra tell — Merchant Huram said — did not Father tell you — "

"Have you been in Damascus all this time? Merchant Huram told Father-in-law that you were not in Damascus, after all."

As we gazed at each other, baffled, Galya came through the vines toward us. Over her shoulder she said, "Go back to the tent, Lila. See if Guri is awake yet."

I started to hold out my arms to Galya, but she folded hers. Looking me up and down, she said, "So, Adara. I wondered if you might be in Damascus, after all. You have done well for yourself."

"God has been good to me," I began. Then my face turned warm, as I understood what Galya must think. "I did not journey from Damascus to visit you,

Stepmother. I came for B'rinna. Is she at the tent?"

Galya shook her head. She wants me to go, I thought. A bit of worry crept into my mind — would B'rinna be willing to come to Damascus with me, especially if the family begged her to stay? But I was determined not to go without seeing B'rinna. At least my foster mother would welcome me.

"Where is B'rinna?" I asked Hannah.

"Oh, Adara." Glancing unhappily at Galya, Hannah shifted the child to her other hip. "A fever went through the town last winter, and B'rinna — B'rinna — "

"B'rinna is dead," said Galya.

I did not want to cry in front of my stepmother, but I could not help myself. As I pressed my headscarf to my face, I felt Hannah's arm around my shoulders.

"B'rinna asked for you at the end," she whispered. "She said, 'Adara has a good heart, no matter what they say. I give her my blessing, wherever she is.'"

"So, Adara," said a man's voice. I dropped my hands from my face and choked down my sobs. My father stood before me. Yes, it was my father, although he did not look nearly as large and powerful as the man I used to imagine rescuing me. His beard was grayer than it had been two years ago, and there were new lines in his forehead.

"So, Father." My tears dried up. I fastened my headscarf over my hair again. Then I untied the bag of silver from my sash. "Sir, I am sorry that I caused you so much worry. I did wrong to go off by myself on the

149

day of the battle. But at least you will not lose my bride price."

My father took the bag, but he looked at it doubtfully. I added, "I earned this money honestly. It is my reward for telling General Naaman of the holy man who healed him."

My father looked more puzzled than before, but he said, "I am not a harsh man. It is well that you have replaced the bride price." Ignoring Galya's anxious look, he went on, "I am a fair man. There is a place for you in my household."

I thought of B'rinna. I gave a sigh that was also one last sob. "No. My place is in another household now. *Shalom*, Father. *Shalom*, Hannah." I turned and walked back through the rows of grapevines.

By the time I reached the caravan, my thoughts had turned toward Damascus. It would be good to see Sima again. I missed her. Now that B'rinna was gone, Sima was my closest friend in the world.

Sima! I stopped at the edge of the road, dazzled by a thought lighting up my mind. I could give my friend something more precious than a dozen bags of silver. I could ask the general for her freedom.

My heart lifted as I pictured Sima's thin face softening with joy. B'rinna seemed to rejoice with us, and so did Elisha.

God gives the solitary a home and brings
forth prisoners into freedom,

I chanted, and I twirled in the steps of a dance.

One of the officers gave me a baffled look. He must still be struggling to understand how a slave girl had brought about the healing of his mighty Lord General Naaman. Laughing, I mounted my donkey. Harness bells jingled and hooves stamped as the caravan got under way again. For the second time in my life, I left my father's vineyard for the northbound road.